"WHY WOULD ANY MAN WANT TO DESTROY YOUR LOVELY, INDOMITABLE SPIRIT?"

Against reason, against wisdom, her face turned toward his in offering. When his eyes asked a question, she did not move away. Their lips met tentatively, then grew bolder, and Jackie felt slightly dizzy as her lips parted involuntarily beneath the pressure of his. There was no denying the instant response of her own betraying body. She had wanted him from the beginning. Forms pressed together, they continued to cling and kiss, desire that was both sweet and wild mounting until all reason was lost in total sensuality . . .

JENNIFER DALE is a writer of a wide variety of fiction, both adult and juvenile. She is also a Certified Medical Assistant. The beautiful Ozarks region of Missouri is home for the author and her husband, two children, and two dogs.

Dear Reader:

Well, this marks the sixth month that we have been publishing Rapture Romance, and the editors have only one thing to say—thank you! At a time when there are so many books to choose from, you have welcomed Rapture Romance, trying our authors, coming back again and again, and writing us of your enthusiasm. Frankly, we're thrilled!

In fact, the response has been so great that we now feel confident that you are ready for more stories which explore all the possibilities that exist when today's men and women fall in love. We are proud to announce that starting this month we will begin publishing four titles each month, because you've told us that two Rapture Romances simply aren't enough. Of course, we will not substitute quantity for quality! We will continue to select only the finest of sensual love stories, stories in which the passionate physical expression of love is the glorious culmination of the entire experience of falling in love.

And please keep writing to us! We love to hear from our readers, and we take your comments and opinions seriously. If you have a few minutes, we would appreciate your filling out the questionnaire at the back of this book, or feel free to write us at the address below. Some of our readers have asked how they can write to their favorite authors, and we applaud their thoughtfulness. Writers need to hear from their fans, and while we cannot give out addresses, we are more than happy to forward any mail.

Happy reading!

Robin Grunder
Rapture Romance
New American Library
1633 Broadway
New York, NY 10019

REMEMBER MY LOVE

by
Jennifer Dale

RAPTURE ROMANCE
NEW AMERICAN LIBRARY
TIMES MIRROR

PUBLISHER'S NOTE

This novel is a work of fiction. Names, characters, places, and incidents are either the product of the author's imagination or are used fictitiously, and any resemblance to actual persons, living or dead, events, or locales is entirely coincidental.

Copyright © 1983 by Jennifer Dale

SIGNET, SIGNET CLASSICS, MENTOR, PLUME, MERIDIAN AND NAL BOOKS are published by The New American Library, Inc., 1633 Broadway, New York, New York 10019

First Printing, July, 1983

1 2 3 4 5 6 7 8 9

PRINTED IN THE UNITED STATES OF AMERICA

Chapter One

"Don't tell me I've already died and gone to heaven," were the first words spoken by Jacqueline Spencer's mysterious patient.

Knowing that reassurance was important at this stage, she smiled and placed her right hand lightly on his arm. When she spoke, her voice was soft and calm. "I wasn't about to tell you any such thing, sir. St. John's Hospital has been described in many ways, but I don't believe 'heavenly' has ever been one of them."

Appearing quite dazed, the reclining man continued to stare at her openly. His eyes did not want to focus properly. No doubt, Jackie thought, this was what had prompted his comment. He was seeing her pretty face and tall, slender form through a bit of a haze, which granted her, from his viewpoint, an ethereal aura.

"St. John's Hospital," he said at last, wrapping his tongue awkwardly around each syllable.

"That's right. Don't struggle with your thoughts. Everything will come back to you quickly now that you're awake, but take it slow and easy. Don't get excited."

He nodded to show he understood, then closed his

eyes. She stood by the hospital bed quietly observing him until he opened them again. As she waited for him to speak she stuffed her stethoscope into one wide pocket of her white coat.

"You're so pretty," he said thickly. "Your eyes . . . so unusual."

Jackie kept on regarding him objectively. She was neither irritated nor flattered by his comments. Since the man was trying to orient himself, she realized he was not making a play for her. In any event, he was not the first patient to be dazzled by her appearance. Looking younger than her thirty years, Jackie *was* undeniably a pretty woman. Her thick hair, dark and lustrous, framed the delicate bone structure of her face, then fell to rest on her shoulders. As the still out-of-balance patient had already observed, her eyes were her most outstanding feature. Long sooty lashes followed the slight slant of her eyes, a characteristic passed down to her from a Japanese grandmother. The surprise came with the color of her eyes, which were a gentian blue, the very unexpectedness of which gave her overall appearance the exotic look of a hothouse orchid.

In addition, she knew she had an unfair advantage over the man. He was seeing her for the first time, and over the past three days, she had observed and examined him twice a day. This was the first time he had regained consciousness since he had been brought to the hospital's emergency room four or five days before. Even with his present pallor and several days' worth of dark stubble on his face, he was a handsome man. Tall and powerfully built, he seemed to fill every inch of the narrow bed. His hair and eyes were both quite dark.

He tried to sit up, groaned loudly, and fell back against the pillow.

"Careful, now," Jackie cautioned. "Remember to take it easy. Don't make any sudden moves."

"Damn, I'm weak. And sore all over. Even my blood hurts. Is that possible?" His voice was low and each word was still pronounced with great deliberation.

"Whatever you say," she replied with a laugh. "It's my job to listen to your symptoms, not assign them."

"Well, then, my blood *does* hurt. Along with everything else. It goes throb, throb, throb, and each throb hurts. What happened to me anyway?"

She gave a deep sigh. "We were all hoping you could tell us that."

"You're my doctor, I assume? At least my luck hasn't been totally bad."

"I'm *one* of your doctors. Several saw you before I did. I got called onto the case because of your failure to regain consciousness. I'm a neurologist. My name, by the way, is Dr. Spencer." She held out her hand and he took it, wincing almost comically at the effort involved in shaking hands. Smiling down at him, she said, "Sorry about that. I forgot about your painful blood condition. Think you can tell us a few things now, Mr—?"

"Us? How many of you are there? I've heard of double vision when you see more than there is, but I've never heard of seeing *less*."

"You can't be too badly off if you're able to make jokes," she told him. "That's purely a professional 'us,' as I'm sure you know, Mr—?"

"Second time you've tried that ploy, Dr. Spencer. I don't believe it's going to work. It isn't that I don't want to cooperate. I just can't seem to come up with a name. You say I've been unconscious. How long?"

"Five days approximately. You were found in an alleyway behind a store. The police found you and brought you here. It's impossible to say how long you had been there."

"Police? Great. Does that mean I'm a criminal?"

"Not necessarily. Just unidentified. As you can see, St. John's isn't a hospital for the elite."

The man's dark eyes, now focusing more properly, assessed his surroundings. Jackie followed the path of his vision. The room, to say the least, was not a place of beauty. The plaster on the walls was cracked and peeling. The faded paint had probably once been a light green, although the layers of grime now covering them made it impossible to be sure. A tired-looking curtain separated him from the patient in the next bed. Everything in the room appeared used, worn out, taped up, and generally dismal.

"I see what you mean, doctor. You're the only bright spot in the joint. I guess this means I'm a charity case, so to speak."

She shrugged. "Until we know. Sounds callous, but it's standard procedure."

"If I can find a Blue Cross card, can I have a better room?" he quipped. He tried to grin but stopped almost immediately, since even that slight use of muscles seemed to cause him discomfort.

"I wouldn't doubt it," she replied lightly. "Maybe even a better doctor."

"No way. That's the only part of this deal I like. No wallet on me?"

"No, nothing, sir. No cars abandoned in the city that could be associated with you. No wallet, money, or business cards. No jewelry. From what I was told, your clothing was cheap, off-the-rack items that couldn't be traced. The theory is that it probably wasn't even yours. It didn't fit and it reeked of cheap wine."

"Great. The answer could be very obvious, you know. Alley, cheap clothes, cheap wine—I'm a bum."

"Somehow I doubt that."

"Thanks."

"Oh, don't thank me. We've checked you out pretty thoroughly. The clothing was filthy but the flesh under it was not. You're obviously in good health. Your teeth and gums are in excellent condition. Mineralization of the bones is good. There are absolutely no signs of the deterioration you would develop with alcoholism and/or malnutrition. Blood samples drawn on your admission here were negative for alcohol. Not even a tiny drop. Are you a teetotaler, do you suppose?"

"How the hell would I know?"

"You're not putting me on, are you? You really don't know who you are?"

"I haven't the foggiest idea, pretty lady. Nothing you've said seems to have any meaning I can connect with myself. Gives me a weird feeling."

"I can imagine it does."

"It's comforting to know I'm not a wino anyway. On the basis of sound medical opinion."

Suddenly he pushed his head deeper into the pillow and laughed. It was the hardiest, healthiest sound he had made and it created a feeling in her she could not define.

"Mind letting me in on the joke?"

"No joke. It suddenly struck me as funny. Perhaps I have a perverted sense of humor. All that evidence you presented . . . throughout it all, I felt a bit uncomfortable. As if I were a specimen rather than a human being, much like one of those plastic models you can see through. It's a rather humbling experience."

"I suppose it is," she said softly. "In fact, I know it is.

Last winter I had a nasty bout with a virus and ended up in a hospital bed. Being a 'specimen,' as you put it, is often more than humbling—it can be humiliating. But I try very hard not to subject my patients to any more of that than is necessary."

"And I'm sure you succeed," he replied, catching hold of her eyes with his. "You've been very considerate and not in the least offensive. And I've already admitted I probably have a perverted sense of humor."

Unable—or unwilling—to move her eyes away from his, she stood there somewhat helplessly. All the words at her command had deserted her, as had her professional objectivity. Because she had been here when he awakened from his coma, because he was without even a sense of self, Jackie felt drawn, and almost protective, toward this stranger. She thought wryly that his terribly good looks didn't hurt either. He gave her a smile that was curiously tender and she was appalled at the sensuality that smile evoked within her. We can't have this, she thought, and the thought was so loud that she felt he surely must have heard it.

Drawing back from his gaze, she returned his smile with a reserved and enigmatic one of her own. Let him make of it what he will, she decided. When she spoke, her voice was cool and low. "Somehow I doubt that anyone could ever humble you."

"Is that based on sound medical opinion or snap judgment?"

"Snap judgment," she admitted, letting herself be charmed into giving him a genuine smile.

He looked around the dismal room again, then gave an exasperated sigh. "What am I to do?"

"I know it's easier to say than to do, but I'd advise you to relax as much as possible. It's sure to come back to you soon. Now, may I disturb your painfully throbbing blood long enough to examine you a little?"

"It's rather nice just talking. But I suppose you'll insist."

"Afraid so."

Jackie pushed the call button to summon a nurse. A middle-aged lady with L. Shipley, R.N. on her starched bosom promptly appeared.

"Now, sir. Just sit up on the edge of the bed. Let your feet dangle. Mrs. Shipley and I are both here to help if needed. Just move slowly."

Jackie carried out her examination, making careful notes on the chart. When she was done, she sighed and shook her head.

"That bad?" he asked anxiously.

"That good. Your Babinski reflex is good. There's no positive Romberg's sign. You heel and toe stand well. Your pupils are the same size and reaction is normal. Funduscopic examination is also perfectly normal."

"Somehow, doctor, you make good sound bad."

She shrugged. "I'm only looking for an explanation for the amnesia. Some amnesia about the events of an accident is common; total amnesia for all past events is a bit more unusual. Obviously you sustained a concussion. X rays for skull fracture were negative, but because you couldn't cooperate and it would have been unwise to move you about too much, the views were limited. As soon as you feel up to it, we'll order a full skull series. Also, it's apparent you were beaten, or something of the sort. Your soreness is due to multiple contusions and muscle spasms."

"You think I'm faking?"

"Not really," she replied. "I do admit the thought crossed my mind. If a person is in trouble, being incognito until the heat's off can be convenient. When you first came to, however, I was fortunate enough to be here. To me, you looked genuinely befuddled. So I'll believe you until it's proved I can't."

"Thanks again." He lay back on the hospital bed and pondered the situation. "I know this will sound dumb to you, but do you suppose that I might recognize myself if I looked in a mirror?"

Jackie gave a small laugh. "I don't know. I suppose it's worth a try. There's a mirror on the back of that tray. Here, we'll push it around to you."

He considered the idea and dismissed it. "I want to get up," he said firmly. "I want to see if I can actually move, not just do those little maneuvers you put me through. Besides, I need to go to the bathroom, so I can look in the mirror in there. I'd really rather not have you two ladies for an audience when I look in the mirror. If it's too bad, I might cry."

"You're pretty enough," said Mrs. Shipley crisply. "You best stay in bed."

The man's outrage was obvious.

"Mrs. Shipley's a good nurse. Better listen," Jackie insisted gently. "You don't need to be up yet. Look in the mirror at hand and we'll get a bedpan for you."

"No way," he announced indignantly. "I want up."

"Then Mrs. Shipley or I stay with you."

"Listen, doctor, what happened to the bit about preserving a patient's humanity and dignity?"

"Really, sir," retorted the nurse, "you've been here several days. Don't you think we've all seen what you've got?"

The look that crossed the man's face was one of the most tragicomic things Jackie had ever seen, a mixture of outrage and murderous intent, defeat and humiliation. She felt her resolve caving in.

"We've done our best, Mrs. Shipley. I think we're dealing with a stubborn man. Just go on and send an orderly in here to help Mr.—our patient."

"I appreciate that," he said softly when the nurse's starched back had disappeared. "I guess my 'modesty' seems ludicrous under the circumstances."

"Not at all."

"It's awkward, isn't it, not to have a name to call me by?"

"Somewhat. But that's only temporary."

The orderly came and assisted the somewhat wobbly patient to the bathroom and back. When he was settled back in the bed, he looked at Jackie rather sheepishly, then thanked the orderly before he left. "I guess I should have listened to you and that dragon of a nurse. I nearly passed out in there."

"Get a chance to look in a mirror?"

"Yeah."

"See anyone you knew?"

"No," he replied glumly. "Just some guy who needs a shave. How about having someone check my fingerprints?"

"That's already been done. If you're a criminal, your prints aren't registered with the police in the city of Biloxi or in the state of Mississippi. Or with the highway patrol or the F.B.I."

"Mississippi? Well, that explains your magnolia-blossom accent. I don't sound like that, do I?"

"You don't make that sound very complimentary," she replied with a laugh. "But, no, you don't have a southern accent. Eastern maybe. I'm not sure. Your speech and accents are educated, even cultured. But not 'magnolia blossom.' "

"Somehow I don't think I'm from anywhere near Mississippi." He sounded quite helpless and dejected.

Jackie looked at her watch and shook her head. "I have to go. There are several other patients I need to see. Are you hungry? I'll ask them to bring you something light to eat. And if you're upset and unable to relax, I'll order a sedative for you."

"I'll take the food. But no thanks on the sedatives. I need to keep what's left of my mind alert."

"Great. Good attitude. Remember to take it as easy as you can."

She turned to leave but his voice stopped her.

"Dr. Spencer?"

"Yes," she said, turning slightly.

"It really does bother me to have no name. What do they call me here? There must be some means of identification for hospital records."

Jackie shook her head a bit sadly. "There has to be. On the floor, you're referred to as the John Doe in 811. On the chart, well . . ." Moving back toward the bed, she showed the cover of the brown chart to him. At its top was written, DOE, MALE PATIENT #947.

He gave a lopsided grin at what he read. "Number nine-four-seven, huh? Not even unique."

"It's a rough world. Lots of transients are brought here to St. John's."

"Well, I can't stand this. Give me a name, Dr. Spencer."

"Pardon?"

"Until I remember, give me a name. Anything, just so I won't be 'sir' and 'hey, you.' "

"Shouldn't you pick your own?"

"I don't know. What's your name—besides 'doctor,' that is?"

"Jackie."

"Jacqueline?"

"Jacqueline Marie."

"That's nice. I like that. Jacqueline Marie."

The way he spoke her name sounded strangely like a caress to her. "But we were discussing *yours*," she reminded him.

"Ah, yes. Male Patient Doe. Not too catchy. Let's see . . . M.P.D. Milford P. Dinglefritz?"

Jackie wrinkled her nose in distaste. "You don't look like a Milford."

"That's one of the nicest things anyone ever said to me."

"That's okay. I was thinking that Mortimer seems somehow more fitting."

"You were thinking that, were you? Well, forget it."

"I will. After all, I still think you should pick out your own. Just think, you can pick Irish, Italian, Hungarian—anything."

"Let's make a deal. I pick the last. You pick the first."

"Fair enough."

"Okay. Dolan."

"Just like that? No deep consideration or heavy thinking? Just 'Dolan' right off the top of your head?"

"Why not? It's only temporary. Has a nice sound to it. Even resembles my present handle of Doe. Now, it's your turn."

"Mark."

"You didn't put much consideration into that either," he pointed out.

"Enough. It's a nice name. Goes well with Dolan. Now, really, I have to go." Even saying that, she did not move away. What was it with this stranger that compelled her to remain with him?

"But you can't leave yet," he said, breaking her train of thought. "We haven't settled the 'P.' "

"That, sir, is entirely your concern."

"You don't have to call me 'sir' anymore. I have a name, remember?"

"I'll try to remember that, *Mark*."

"Mark who?"

"I give up . . . Mark who?"

"Mark Patrick. Mark Patrick Dolan." He seemed almost childishly pleased with himself.

"Good. See you around, Mark."

"When will you be back? Again today?"

There was a compelling appeal in his voice. All through their seemingly playful banter, there had been an undercurrent of strong emotion, a curious reluctance to part. Her sympathy flowed out to the man. He was undergoing a very frightening experience and was bearing it with strength and humor. There was much to admire in that. Yet it was not only sympathy that held her in this room and she realized this fully.

"I suppose I could come back tonight right before I go home. You might have remembered something by then."

"It might be wise for you to stay with me."

"Why's that?" she asked, the beginnings of a smile at the corners of her mouth. It was impossible not to like the man.

"We seem to get along well with me being Mark. A few hours from now, I might have remembered and will be someone else entirely. We should seize these few moments while we have them."

"Uh-uh. You try telling that to my other patients. Now, doctor's orders, sit back and relax. I'll order your food." On the way out the door, she looked back at him and smiled impishly. "You know what I think, Mr. Dolan?"

"No, what do you think, Dr. Spencer?"

"With the line of repartee you have, you must be a game-show host. Run that through your memory and see if it rings any bells." She did not look back at him but his laughter followed her down the long, sterile hospital corridor and echoed in her mind even longer.

As she went about her hospital rounds she saw a few of the other physicians and advised them that their newest John Doe had regained consciousness. After she had seen her last patient and dictated all of her progress notes, she went to the doctors' lounge for a cup of coffee. Dr. Vonkleman, a staff psychiatrist, joined her there.

"I saw the patient in eight-eleven. He tells me you helped him pick out a name." The older man seemed slightly amused.

Jackie shrugged. "He insisted. Right now he's going through a very bewildering experience. What do you think of him, doctor?"

"Well-developed, well-nourished Caucasian male appearing to be approximately thirty-five years of age."

"You know what I mean, Harv," she said dryly.

"Yeah, well, you know me. I put him through the paces. Tried to trip him up every way possible. He wouldn't trip. In my opinion, the amnesia's real enough."

"No guesses on how long it might last?"

"Not at this stage of the game."

"Any suggestions?"

She regarded the older doctor silently as he considered the matter. At last he shook his head, causing a strand of gray hair to fall across his forehead. "We could try hypnosis. Usually it doesn't work, but once in a while it does. It's worth a try. But what he really needs is time. That's what it'll take to bring him around."

Putting down her coffee cup, Jackie prepared to leave.

"Done for the day?" Vonkleman asked.

"No such luck. I still have to go by the free clinic over on Marley Boulevard. They've scheduled a couple of examinations over there for me. And if it goes as it usually does, I'll see a dozen patients before I get out of the place."

"Thought this was Mendoza's week to do neurology there."

"It is. We traded. He has a golf tournament."

Vonkleman laughed and shook his head. "You're a born sucker, Jackie. They all take advantage of you because of your soft heart."

"I think you mean soft head."

"You could always say 'no.' "

"That's true. Still, it's less complicated for me. No husband, no kids, no frail and aged relatives."

"And why's that?"

"My parents are still quite young and active."

"You know that's not what I'm asking."

She tossed back her dark hair and laughed. "I know. And you know the answer anyway."

"I do?"

"Sure you do. How would you like to marry me?"

"I'm already married to Betty," he replied lamely.

"And is Betty much like me?"

"Not much."

"That's what I thought."

"Hey," he protested when he saw she was on her way out the door. "I don't get it."

"Just think about it. You'll figure it out."

Jackie left to go to her car. Some days Vonkleman's

sense of humor was a bit too much. Her singleness, which he questioned, was something she accepted as a permanent condition. Her combination of beauty, brains, dedication, and ambition were a bit too much for the average male. All the men she had come even close to being serious with always expected her to alter her life-style drastically when married. But Jackie had chosen to be a doctor, and a patient in need would always come before any man's need for a hot meal or a wife in his bed. When and if she met a man capable of understanding that her dedication did not diminish the love they could share, then she would consider marriage. But she didn't expect that to happen. Male doctors expected their wives to understand. Funny how it was all so different when the situation was reversed.

Once she had entered the free clinic and started her examinations there, all thoughts of her personal life slid away. Just as she had predicted, the few patients had blossomed into many. It was dark and well past dinner time when she finally got away. She patted her growling tummy, an act which didn't comfort it much. No wonder she had no trouble staying slender; there was never time to eat, she thought unhappily. She was beginning to regret that she had promised Mark she would come back to the hospital. There was no other reason to go. She could call and have someone tell him she had been "unavoidably detained" and would see him on morning rounds the next day. Only for some reason, despite her exhaustion, Jackie felt compelled to go.

Her small car seemed to make the turns back to St. John's without any conscious effort on her part. As if, she thought wryly, even the car knew what a glutton for punishment she was.

After she had slipped into her white coat once more, she rode the elevator to the eighth floor. Going to the nurses' station, she took Male Patient Doe's chart from the rack. She read over it quickly before going to his room. Several other physicians had seen him during the day and noted their findings. Apparently his memory had not yet returned.

The room was dark when she entered. She smiled at the elderly man in the bed by the window. He was reading a newspaper by the light of a small lamp on his bedside table. The curtain was still drawn between him and the younger man, who appeared to be sleeping.

"Has he been asleep long?" Jackie inquired of the man. She was feeling somewhat hesitant about waking up "Mark."

The man returned her smile but shrugged and spoke a phrase in Spanish to indicate he did not understand her question. Jackie took a few steps toward her patient's bed and could no longer see the other man. When Mark opened his eyes and gave her a long, grave look, she was greatly relieved.

"I'm so glad to see you're awake, Mr. Dolan. I had promised I would come by and didn't want to leave without seeing you, but I wouldn't have wanted to wake you. I'm sure you've had a tiring day."

"To say the least. I think every physician in the state of Mississippi has looked into my eyes and tapped my kneecaps today."

"That's what you get for being such an interesting case."

Mark sat up in the bed, plumping the pillow up behind his back. He reached over and flipped on his light. Jackie noticed that he was moving more surely already. His physical recovery was going to be no problem, she thought. All they had to do was get his memory to function.

"Speaking of tired," he said, "that's how *you* look. Busy day?"

"Very much so. I made rounds here this morning, then was in my office till midafternoon, though I was just supposed to be there half a day; then I came back here, after which I went to see patients at the free clinic. I just finished there before I came here."

"Now you're making me feel guilty for asking you to come back."

She gave a dismissing shrug. "As I said, you're an interesting case. I wanted to see how the memory was doing."

"It isn't." He seemed remarkably unconcerned at the moment.

"Ah, well. You *are* looking quite fit, though."

He beamed at her, his recently scrubbed and shaved face looking boyish. "Glad you noticed. Takes a lot of trust to be in this place. Strange people coming at me with razors and other sadistic-appearing equipment. But I've survived."

"I predict you'll keep on doing that."

"Put that in writing?"

"Never," she said with a laugh. "I'm much too cautious for that."

"Is caution why you're not married?"

She lowered her brows and looked at him closely before she replied. "How do you know I'm not?"

"I've inquired here and there."

"I see. Would you believe you're the second person to question my single state today? Actually, though, caution has nothing to do with it. It has more to do with the schedule I outlined to you a few moments ago."

"No time for love? All work and no play . . ."

"Hush with the platitudes, Mr. Dolan. You didn't ask about 'play,' you asked about marriage. From what I understand, they're not one and the same. And I don't think you get the point anyway. Not that it matters. After all, it isn't *me* we have to find out about—it's you."

"True. But I didn't think it would hurt to ask."

"Any particular reason why it mattered?" She kept her voice light but was acutely aware of a fluttering sensation of pulse against her jacket cuffs. This man was a mystery to her in more ways than one. Like the idea or not, she was intrigued. And not just by the medical aspects of his case.

"Typical woman, fishing for compliments. I've already told you I find you attractive. Isn't that reason enough?"

"Perhaps. Yet it's scarcely pertinent."

"Meaning . . .?"

"We don't know about your marital state. Or anything else."

"So I could have a big, fat wife and thirteen kids?"

"That's right." He seemed quite dejected by the idea. "On the other hand," Jackie continued, "she—your wife, that is—could be slender and beautiful."

Even that thought didn't seem to cheer him. "Would you like to place bets on my marital status?"

"No way," she said with a laugh. "You don't act married. But a lot of married men don't act married. We'll just have to wait and see."

"Well, I'm hoping I'm not. Because when I get out of here, I'd like to ask you out. To thank you for being kind, for coming back to see me tonight when you're obviously exhausted."

"Totally unnecessary. Because, if I find out you're rich, I'll send you an exorbitant bill, and if you pay it, that'll be thanks enough."

"Mercenary woman."

"Of course."

Although their tones were light, Jackie knew herself well enough to feel uneasy. She was hoping this man wasn't married. She was hoping that, somehow, he could be hers, that, like Sleeping Beauty in reverse, he would recover, and that he would be different from the other men she had known, that he could see what she was and love her anyway without asking her to change drastically. Yet she knew that such thoughts, even drifting idly across the mind's surface, were dangerous. They threatened professional objectivity. And they also threatened emotional security.

"Really," she said, putting on her reserve and bedside manner, "you still don't recall anything at all?"

He shook his head regretfully. "I do, however, have an almost uncontrollable urge for a cheeseburger with onions and Coca-Cola over crushed ice. I suppose that could be construed as a memory of sorts. If I want them, I must remember liking them. That food you had sent to me—it was better than nothing, but not by much. Jello and broth? Now, is that any kind of meal for a grown man?"

Jackie nodded her head solemnly. "It's appropriate fare for a grown man who has taken nothing by mouth for several days. It's highly likely that a cheeseburger with onions would have had an unsettling effect on your gastrointestinal system."

"When do I get food, then?"

"I can order another light meal for you, if you'd like,

before you settle in for the night. If that stays down all right, we'll put you on a regular diet tomorrow."

"Could we maybe . . .?" The question died in midair and Mark leaned his handsome head back against the pillow.

"Yes?" she coaxed.

He offered her a slightly sheepish grin. "I was going to ask you if you'd consider at least walking with me to the hospital cafeteria where we could get a light snack. Then several things occurred to me. I have no money. I have no clothes. And you'd probably consider it a breech of professional etiquette in any event."

"Professional etiquette? I might consider it that, I guess. But you can't go parading around in the cafeteria yet, not even if you had a whole closetful of Brooks Brothers suits and a Diner's Club card. But to tell you the truth—and putting professional etiquette aside—I'm half starved myself. That cheeseburger sounds appealing."

"Yeah, well, the big difference is that you'll leave me here and go have one. And someone will bring me a tray of unidentifiable pap. It's unfair."

"Life often is."

A moment of awkwardness descended upon them, a moment that shouldn't occur between doctor and patient, though it often did between a man and a woman.

She tapped her ophthalmoscope nervously, then placed it in her pocket. "I do have to leave now. When I pass the desk, I'll ask them to bring you some 'pap.' Then I'll see you in the morning. Very early. Perhaps, after a good night's rest, your mind will open up to all sorts of things."

"If you say so. Good night, pretty lady."

"Good night, Mr. Dolan."

"Mark."

"Mark. Good night."

Jackie had every intention of going straight home and eating something there. Often she popped a frozen dinner in the oven while she soaked her weary body in hot, fragrant water. But she was terribly hungry, and as she passed the hospital's snack bar, the aroma from the grill was irresistible.

"Late hours and improper meals again, Dr. Spencer," chided Millie, the snack-bar employee who took her order.

"Is that any way to refer to the food you serve?" Jackie retorted.

The woman was unruffled. "Nothing wrong with the food I serve. But you need some good vegetables and fruit, too. Being a doctor, you should know that."

"I watch my diet," she began to protest.

"Uh-uh," the woman interrupted. "Today, for instance . . . was it well balanced?"

Jackie thought back guiltily to the sweet roll for breakfast and the burrito purchased from a cart for lunch. "Okay," she told Millie with a smile, "I've been remiss. But tomorrow I'll do better."

"No, tonight you'll do better," Millie replied firmly. The platter she placed in front of Jackie held a delicious-looking salad as well as the cheeseburger she had ordered; the cola drink she had specified had been replaced by a glass of milk.

"Millie, you're working in the wrong place. They need you in the dietary department."

"I know where I'm needed, doctor. In dietary, *you* do the ordering. Here I do."

Millie got busy with other customers and Jackie turned her attention to her meal. After a few bites, her pleasure in it diminished. She kept thinking of the wistfulness that had appeared in a pair of brown eyes when cheeseburgers were discussed.

"Millie," she called, "I'd like another cheeseburger and milk, fixed to go."

"You *are* hungry."

Not bothering to explain, Jackie only smiled. By the time she had finished her own meal, Millie had placed a white paper bag in front of her. On the way back up to 811, Jackie began to feel something like a fool. What she was doing would be understandable if her patient were a child. But Male Patient Doe was no child and her concern could easily be misinterpreted. But then, again, she'd be among the first to admit she wasn't sure what the proper interpretation of this situation would be.

When she stood once more in Mark's room, she was as shy as a schoolgirl. Mark's eyes brightened when he saw her. She wasn't sure if this was due to her presence or the aroma that escaped from the paper bag.

"I gave in," she said meekly.

"You're being very kind to me."

"Aren't I, though? Beware, I'll be expecting something in return. Want to take a walk? You shouldn't go far, but there's a place just down the hall where you can sit and watch the traffic below."

Mark sat up in bed eagerly, pulled at his hospital gown, and then fell back in disgust. "Back to the issue of no clothes."

"St. John's provides for its patients well," Jackie told him. From the narrow closet on his side of the room, she took a limp robe and a pair of ugly house slippers. All items were marked conspicuously with the hospital logo and name.

"Sorry-looking things, aren't they?" he commented.

However, he took the garments and put them on without argument.

"You're doing quite well," she said as they walked slowly down the hospital corridor. "You seem very steady. Any dizziness or nausea?"

He shook his head negatively. "I still hurt all over. Otherwise, I feel fine."

A few minutes later, cheeseburger devoured, he sat on the broad window seat and looked eight stories down. The highway below was busy, each vehicle sending out streams of yellow light as it passed. Across from the highway was a small park, its fountain-centered lake sparkling prettily under the artificial lighting. "Biloxi, Mississippi," he said. "What a place to end up."

"It's not a bad city."

"Oh, I'm sure it's not. No place, however, is too appealing from inside a hospital. On the riverfront it's a picturesque city, I suppose?"

"Very much so. Colonial-style houses, riverboats, barges."

"*The Mississippi Gambler*," he said softly.

"See?" she said, quite pleased. "You remember snatches of things here and there. You know what might be a good idea?"

"What's that? Another cheeseburger maybe?"

"Don't push your luck. I went against my better medical judgment with the first one. No, I wasn't thinking of food. More of books and such. Perhaps reading different things will help ring some bells, summon up some memories. I'll see what I can do about getting some books and magazines up here for you tomorrow."

"You're terribly kind, doctor."

She shrugged. "I keep telling you what an interesting case you are. Maybe that's what I meant when I said I was expecting something in return. Like a medical exclusive. You sign over all rights to your case to me and I'll write you up in some long-winded medical journal and become famous."

"You expect all that for a mere cheeseburger?"

"It doesn't hurt to dream, does it?"

"Never."

Jackie had meant to keep her distance, both emotionally and physically. Somehow or other, though, she ended up standing over Mark, her hand on his shoulder, while they stood watching the movements of Biloxi at night in a companionable silence. She wasn't sure how or when her hand had moved to his shoulder, yet, noting it, she left it there.

"All those people moving about down there. So many of them . . . and they all know who they are and where they're going. They don't even think about it, don't know how lucky they are."

"Don't get down about it, Mark. It seems longer, but it's only been a few hours since you regained consciousness. I'm sure it's frustrating for you, but try not to be discouraged."

"Someone down there did this to me." His voice was rather matter-of-fact.

"Yes. Out there anyway—somewhere in the world."

He stood up suddenly and towered over her. His eyes were puzzled and hurt, and Jackie had to fight off a curious urge to touch him again in some comforting gesture. Although she did not give in to the urge, Mark almost seemed to sense its presence. Smiling tenderly, the bitterness dropped away from his face. "It could be worse, doctor—much worse. You're right, of course. In time, it will all come back. And now, as much as I like having you here, I think you should go home. You look very tired."

"I am," she admitted, inordinately pleased at his consideration. "Let's walk back toward your room, then I'll go home."

"Be careful out there."

"I will. Have good dreams."

"I'll try, Dr. Spencer. Who knows, maybe I'll even dream about myself."

"If you do, remember to let me know first. My exclusive rights."

"You bet."

Weary though she was, she hated to leave Mark Patrick Dolan. She was undeniably drawn to the man. On the way home, she managed to convince herself this was a combination of sympathy for his plight and medical curiosity. She was quite convinced she would feel the same way if he were ugly or old. But it made for a nice bonus that he wasn't.

Chapter Two

"Where are you going with that load of stuff?" Dr. Vonkleman asked Jackie.

She glanced down at the heap of magazines and books in her arms almost guiltily. When she spoke, however, it was without a trace of apology. "Just a few things to give our amnesia victim to read. Who knows, something might jar his memory, give him a key to his identity or profession."

"It's worth a try. Some of these retrograde cases can be stubborn, though."

"How long does it generally last? Can you give me any clues at all, Harv?"

He shrugged. "Hours, days, weeks, months, years. Take your pick. I've seen it happen all ways. Often patients *never* regain the memory of the traumatizing event. They can recall everything before and after but never the event itself."

"But total amnesia for *all* past events? Have you known a case where that persisted for years—or forever?"

"Something will come back to the young man, Jackie. If you'd like, I'll hypnotize him in a day or two. See what happens then."

"Great. Whenever you think he's ready, try it. Too much of this and he's going to get depressed on us. So far he's been remarkably calm about the situation, but I know it's frightening."

"True, but he's had a few breaks. Like your personalized attention. When a man has you around taking an interest in him, it wards off depression nicely. At least I think it would."

"Personalized attention," she asked, lifting her eyebrows quizzically. "He's just a patient like any other."

"Sure he is, Jackie. Sure he is." He went on off down the corridor, his laughter booming after him. Jackie felt both irritated and disturbed. Had her attraction to the man been so very obvious? The idea of it served as a warning to her.

Mark's pleasure in seeing her, and his gratitude at the reading material she had brought, was touching. He seemed so lonely that she hated to leave him. Watch it, Jackie, she warned herself. Taking too much pity on an attractive man can be lethal when he was so totally an unknown quantity.

"You talk to your roommate any?" she asked on her way out.

"Enough to know I'm not bilingual," he answered dryly.

"I know one thing about you, Mark. . . ."

"And that is?"

"You speak English well and have a good vocabulary. There could be a key there."

"Maybe I'm a writer or an English teacher."

"Could be. Keep your mind working."

Jackie saw the rest of her patients at St. John's and then returned to her office. Her day was, as always, quite busy. She had several new patients to evaluate in addition to many routine checkups. Being a good doctor, her mind was on her patients and how she could best serve them. Yet Mark Dolan was never really out of her mind. The thought of him rested there, lightly, almost imperceptibly. When she took a break to drink a cup of coffee, she found herself smiling at the mental picture of his boyish delight with the cheeseburger. If she closed her eyes for a moment's rest, she could see his face, the mischievous glint in his brown eyes, as clearly as if he were with her.

"You're awfully quiet today," Sharon, her office nurse, commented.

"I've been too busy to talk," she replied with a smile. *Too busy thinking about a man I have no business thinking about.*

It was late afternoon before she got back to St. John's. She found she had been asked by another physician to see a new patient, a small girl who had been having a series of convulsive seizures. The child was a timid six-year-old and Jackie spent a long time with her, simply trying to gain her confidence before the actual examination. After she had written up her findings, she went to Mark's room. Quite on purpose, she did not see her other patients first. She wanted an excuse for not staying with him long.

"Any progress?" she asked.

"None at all."

"I see." Very briskly and clinically, she ran a few tests on him. He was disgustingly normal. When she informed him of that fact, he did not seem too pleased.

"I suppose I want some logical explanation, some concrete reason why I am the way I am."

"There's been a severe shock to your system, Mark. Even if there are no obvious clinical findings, there has definitely been some damage. Do you have any objections to hypnosis?"

His entire face brightened at the thought. The easy grin with which she was becoming quite familiar widened. "Sounds like a great idea. Surely my subconscious mind doesn't have amnesia too."

"Don't get your hopes up too high, Mark," she warned. "It doesn't work more often than it works."

"You're a big help," he retorted. "Well, when do we start on this new endeavor?"

"*We* don't. I won't be doing the hypnosis. Dr. Vonkleman will."

"Another neurologist?"

"Psychiatrist."

"Charming thought."

"Don't be prejudiced. Anyway, no one is saying you're crazy, but you can't argue with the fact that you have a mental disorder of sorts. He's a good psychiatrist and he's had a lot of training and experience with hypnosis. Cooperate?"

"Of course. Only I don't suppose he's as pretty as you are?"

"Depends on the point of view. Well, now, I have other patients to see. I'll get a message to Vonkleman. And, by the way, you've met him. He's been in here since you woke up."

"Who hasn't? Most of them didn't bother with introductions. They merely probed and poked. If I had my Blue Cross card, they wouldn't treat me like this."

"Then you better keep looking. Good night."

"Good night. Tell me one thing before you go, Dr. Spencer. . . ."

"Surely."

"You're different tonight. Very cool. Totally professional."

"And?"

"And . . . nothing, really. I just liked the other version of you better. Is there a reason for the change?"

"That other side of me . . . It gets me in trouble at times."

"Careful there, doctor. You might be making an admission." His eyes moved up and down, apparently perceiving each curve of her slender form beneath the white coat.

She shifted position slightly and looked straight at him. "I try to be honest, with my patients and with myself. You're an attractive man and I enjoy your company. Considering everything, it would be wise to be wary, don't you think?"

"Wise? Definitely it would be wise. And dull."

"The story of my life. Now, good night."

"As you wish. Good night."

Early the next morning Jackie talked to several other physicians, and they agreed that hypnosis should be tried next on Mark Dolan. Dr. Vonkleman said he would start the procedure right away, before he went to his private office. Because of this, Jackie did not go to see Mark. She was almost glad for the excuse. Harv Vonkleman called her in the afternoon and reported that the hypnosis had produced no significant findings. The radiologist had looked at the complete skull X-ray series and pronounced it to be completely within normal limits. The EEG and CAT scan were also negative. Poor Mark, she thought. Everything was working so well . . . except his memory.

Between patients, she read from her medical textbooks to refresh her knowledge of amnesia. We know so much, she thought, as she closed the pages of one thick volume, and yet so much remains a mystery.

When she went back to the hospital for evening rounds, she talked to some of the other doctors who had examined Mark at various times. Everyone was intrigued by his case, yet no one had any suggestions to offer to hasten his recovery. The police had run his picture in most major newspapers but no one had called them with any information.

"You still don't think it's epilepsy on little Amy Shortell?" Dr. Hamilton asked her.

"No, Gary, I don't. I'll be glad to look in on her again if you'd like. But the seizures seem drug-induced to me."

"She's on no regular medications."

"Drugs of the illicit sort, perhaps."

"Jackie, really, the child is only six. And her family seems to be good, stable."

"You asked my opinion. I gave it. You'll do as you like, of course, but I'd certainly recommend a blood screening. And as soon as possible. Wait any longer and it'll be out of her system."

"Will do," he said with a shrug, "but it's a bit like chasing shadows."

"Ah, but if you ever catch one, it will be worth all the effort."

"Jackie, you're something else. And, speaking of chasing shadows, what direction are you taking now on your John Doe?"

"I don't know. I really don't. Right now I suppose I'll go see him, go over his chart with him, let him know what all my fine colleagues think of the situation."

*   *   *

Jackie entered Room 811 with some hesitation. What do you say to a man who has no memory at all? All the platitudes about time and patience had been uttered. She suspected they offered little comfort to Mark Dolan.

"Well, well, the lost have returned. You were conspicuously absent this morning, doctor. More cooling off needed?"

"You're not going to let me forget that, are you?" Jackie commented with a laugh. "As I recall, you were being hypnotized this morning. I didn't have time to wait until Dr. Vonkleman was done. Did you find the experience interesting?"

Mark's laugh was brief and mirthless. "Interesting? Perhaps. I did as I was told—let my mind stroll down country lanes. I'm told I remembered nothing of consequence. And the experiment made me miss your visit. All in all, it wasn't worth the effort."

"We had to try."

"I know. I'm just being a clod."

"That's understandable. It's a difficult situation."

"What next?" His keen eyes searched her face as if hoping to find the answers written there.

"I suppose that's what I'm here to discuss with you."

"Have a seat then," he said, patting the edge of his bed. Jackie ignored the gesture and pulled up an ancient chair. She was determined to keep her distance, physically and emotionally. Getting involved with a man who had no past—or, worse yet, a past filled with previous commitments—was a risk she couldn't let herself take. As simply as possible, she explained his tests and their results and relayed the opinions of the other physicians. In regard to his amnesia, the findings were not favorable and he seemed to get that message quite clearly.

"It's a difficult thing to deal with, Mark. Most medical disorders show up on X rays and laboratory tests. We can see the problem, treat it, recheck it to see if it's cleared up. Your nervous system—*everyone's* nervous system—contains limbic structures for storage of memory. The injury you suffered has caused some change in the molecular structure of these 'memory storage units.' The memories are still there but the problem is in getting through the 'damaged containers' to retrieve them. There have been some cases of seemingly permanent metabolic amnesia syndrome which have improved slowly over the years."

"You're not being encouraging, Dr. Spencer."

"All I'm trying to do right now is to explain what the problem is so you can understand it."

"Very good. You may continue."

"As we've told you before, most posttraumatic amnesia is short-term and generally involves loss of memory for events surrounding the injury only."

"And I had to go and be different."

"I'm afraid so," Jackie said sympathetically. Once more she felt a twinge of admiration for this man who retained his sense of humor even as he learned he might never regain his memory. "You've already shown an ability to learn new material and store it. This proves your damage is purely retrograde, or retroactive. When the memory unit itself is affected, new material cannot be retained for more than a few seconds."

"So I can go forward, but not back."

"Yes. I rather suspect you will begin to remember some things soon. Even so, after a period of around three months, if you have not fully recovered, it's possible you might never. Not fully. Whether *your* amnesia is transient or permanent remains to be seen. But the information is there, Mark, in those limbic structures. It's a matter of retrieving it. Any questions?"

He put his head down in his hands for a few seconds without speaking. "And there's no treatment?" he asked at last.

She was touched by the calmness in his voice. "No," she replied reluctantly. "Lots of research is being done, but there is no real evidence at this point that *any* therapy is effective in restoring memory disorders."

He looked at her directly, parted his lips as if to speak, then let them close again.

"You wanted to ask something else? I'll explain anything I can. If you'd like, I'll bring material for you to read on the subject. Although I warn you, the technical jargon can be confusing."

"Then don't bring it," he said wryly. "I'm confused enough as it is."

"Really, Mark, please ask anything you want. I'll try to help."

"I know you'll try, dear doctor. But I was all prepared to ask 'what do I do now' and then I realized you can't answer that. It's my problem."

"You'll be here awhile yet. After that, you'll be helped in some way. Believe me, you won't just be turned out onto the streets of Biloxi without a name or a dollar."

"I suppose I should be comforted by that."

She watched him sitting there on the narrow bed, the snowy white sheet across his knees, and a strange emotion welled up within her. "Dammit, Mark," she blurted out, "you don't have to be so brave and calm. You can cry or cuss or fly into a terrible rage. You have the right to vent some of the frustration you must be feeling." In saying that, she knew her resolve to maintain emotional detachment had flown right out the window.

He looked at her quizzically, a half smile on his face. "Would it help if I did all that?"

"I don't know," she admitted. "It wouldn't help the amnesia. Maybe it would help your spirits."

For modesty's sake, he picked up the faded hospital robe from the end up his bed, slipped it on, and got out of bed. "Take a short walk with me?" he asked. "Maybe back to our window. See what the ducks on the lake are up to."

After they had stood at the window awhile, he spoke without looking at her. "You know, fair doctor, I've felt like doing all those things you mentioned: crying, cursing, throwing things, breaking the whole world around me to bits. But I can't do any of them. Somehow I just can't. It's hard to explain, but I feel totally dependent, very helpless. It's like being a small child who wants to throw a tantrum but is afraid to because he fears the consequences, needs Mommy's help. For a grown man, it's a terrible feeling to have."

"There's a helplessness in my feelings, too, Mark. I spent so many years studying and working so I could help people, yet so often there's little I can do. Look at it this way, if you can: you're obviously an intelligent man and your ability to comprehend and store new material is good. Even if you never learn who you *were*, you can build a future."

"Mark Patrick Dolan. Born at the age of . . . see, I don't even know that much. This future I'm to build . . . with what? With whom?"

"Mark, we'll find a way."

"We?"

She knew she should not have committed herself, yet she was driven by a compassion so intense that she could not hold back the words. "Yes, *we*. I'll find a way to help you somehow."

He turned toward her. Reaching out, he placed a hand on each of her shoulders. She had not expected his touch, and it seemed to burn a place through the fabric of her white coat and the soft blouse beneath it. Dark eyes met light and held. Neither of them spoke. There did not appear to be any words appropriate for the occasion. She felt content and happy within his light touch. The moment had nothing to do with logic and reason.

"This help you offer," he said quietly, "can you tell me if it comes from the doctor or from the woman?"

"I don't know," she replied truthfully. "In fact, I think we're inseparable."

"That's good."

"Is it?" A trace of bitterness edged her words. "I've often been told it isn't good at all."

"The man lucky enough to get you, my dearest doctor, cannot claim you with the intent of conquering you. Why would a man even *want* to destroy your lovely, indomitable spirit?"

Against reason, against wisdom, she knew her face was turned toward him in offering. When his eyes asked a question, she did not move away. Their lips met tentatively, then grew bolder, and Jackie felt slightly dizzy as her lips parted involuntarily beneath the pressure of Mark's. There was no denying the instant response of her own self-betraying body. She had wanted him from the beginning and the runaway emotion she experienced within his embrace offered no discouragement to her desire. Logic, where are you when I need you most, she thought . . . and then all thoughts were silenced by his increasingly demanding kiss.

Stunned by the impact he had on her, Jackie nonetheless managed to withdraw from his embrace, although his hands were still firmly planted on her shoulders.

"This isn't very professional," she managed to say.

"No, but nice."

She neither denied nor admitted, but said, "We can't do this again. There are too many things we don't know."

"We know how we feel about each other."

"At this point, that's not enough, Mark."

"I know."

They gazed into each other's eyes for a moment longer, and then he removed his hands. Jackie was almost shocked by the feeling of loss she suffered instantaneously. She had told him no lie. Where this man was concerned, the doctor and the woman were inextricably entangled. She had promised to help him and had to do so. But she warned herself to make certain her help was tempered with a large measure of common sense. Her future could not include this man in any capacity except that of patient and casual acquaintance. The man was an amnesia victim . . . her patient. Letting him get too dependent on her at this point could well be a breach of professional etiquette. And even without that to consider, there were so many problems. Who was he, really, and what was he? As her own treacherous heart was telling her, he was awfully easy to love. Somewhere there could be a woman crying and aching because he had not returned home. No, she could not have dreams of Mark Dolan. His past could hold too many obstacles.

"You can't mean that," Jackie said indignantly. She looked around the long conference table at the rows of faces hoping to find even one face that mirrored her own outrage. The other doctors' expressions, however, were all guarded and closed. No kindred spirit sat on this review committee.

"Look at the situation logically, Dr. Spencer," said the heavyset physician who had uttered the verdict that sparked her comment. "The man is physically fit. He's a total charity case. You know his bed is needed for a more acutely ill patient."

"So we just throw him out in the street," she retorted with bitterness. "He has no identity, no family or friends to contact, no money, and no way of making a living. What's the man to do?"

"Contact a social worker, doctor. That's their job, not ours."

"You know what they'll do with him?" she asked. Several of her colleagues looked uncomfortable but no one answered. "Well, I can tell you what a social worker will do with him. He'll be placed in a sheltered work-shop environment."

"Is there something wrong with that?" someone asked.

"This man is different," she insisted. "He's obviously intelligent and educated. What is he going to learn in a place like that? They have a good purpose, heaven knows I believe that. But not for Mark Dolan. He's capable of so much more."

"Is he, Jackie?" Harv Vonkleman dared to say. "Sure, he's nice-looking and personable. But who's going to hire him to head up their corporation? A man with no name, no references, no background? I hate to say it, my dear, but you're getting too personally involved in this case. The review committee has decided that Male Patient Doe number nine-four-seven will be discharged within two days. Is that understood?"

"That's understood very well."

"Good. Next case?"

Jackie sat through the rest of the meeting fidgeting and fuming. She had told Mark she would help him, but she hadn't expected the need for help to come this soon. Sure, she agreed with the medical opinion that he had recovered physically, but it seemed so heartless to dismiss him to social services and forget about him.

She broke the news to him that evening. He was very calm and accepting. All the fury had been hers.

"It's to be expected," he said, sensing her outrage. "I'm healthy and strong. I know the bed is needed for someone who is actually sick."

"Now you sound like that idiot on the review committee," she snapped.

He laughed at her irritation. "I'll find something to do, don't worry. I know there isn't much in my head at present, but my back is strong. Maybe I can find a construction job or something."

"No, you can't."

"Why on earth not?"

"Who are you going to tell them you are? They'll want a social security number. And the social security administration won't issue you one without proof of identity. And if you had proof of identity, you'd already have a social security card and thus probably wouldn't need a construction job."

"Is that one of those fabled vicious circles?"

"I believe it just might be."

She looked at him carefully and shook her head. "Well, you think about it and I'll think about it. I'll contact a social worker and see if someone somewhere has an idea. Then I'll get back to you."

"Okay, just don't stay away too long."

"Be back tonight. We have to come up with something.

Tomorrow you'll be officially discharged from St. John's Hospital."

"Even with all the problems, that doesn't sound too bad. It's getting to be a bit of a drag in here."

After Jackie and Mark exchanged farewells, she went on to her office. From there, she took time out from her busy schedule to call various people, offices, and agencies. She even took a few minutes between office hours and her schedule at the free clinic to go talk to the director of the social services program at St. John's. By the end of the day, she was gritting her teeth in frustration.

One social worker suggested that Mark apply for state assistance—a welfare program—until his identity could be discovered. During a telephone conversation with a worker from the county welfare office, Jackie discovered that Mark's residence would have to be known before he was eligible. Even if he were to be considered a current resident of Mississippi, they needed his prior state of residence for their records. An office that worked on vocational rehabilitation assured her that they would make every effort to find a field suited to his capabilities. However, they too needed information that was simply not available, as would any prospective employer.

She felt so dismal that she dared not go near Mark. When she went by St. John's before going home, she saw her other patients and left a message with the eighth-floor nurses' station to be delivered to Mark. One way or another, she was going to have something worked out for him the next day.

Bright and early the next morning, she cornered the hospital administrator. "Can't you give him a job here, Mr. Gallen? Anything at all? It would just be a temporary measure until we can get some red tape untangled.

The poor man has to have some way to make a little money."

"Aren't there social programs, Dr. Spencer?"

"There are, but that's where the red tape lies. He's not eligible to apply for anything until he has proof of identity. There has to be a way to find out who he is, and that's what I'm working on."

"I don't mean to criticize you, Dr. Spencer—in fact, I admire your attitude—but you're too busy to involve yourself in this matter so deeply. We have a pretty good program of social aid here. Turn your John Doe over to them. They won't let him starve."

"There's more to life than bread and meat," she muttered.

"Look, I understand what you're trying to do. I'd like to help you, but I don't see how. St. John's has 'red tape' for prospective employees too. We have to have references for his file, a social security number before we can pay him. Those are *laws*, doctor, not just silly rules."

"I know, I know. And I don't mean to put you in an awkward position. Okay, then, how about unofficial work for you personally?"

"Pardon?"

"Leaf raking, house painting, cleaning out garages, washing your car—give him jobs where he's paid in cash. Small sums. And spread the word among your friends. Just enough to make him feel a bit self-sustaining until we can work out something better. What do you say?"

Jackie gave the administrator the full force of her smile. Although most men were a bit intimidated by her, she was well aware that they were not immune to her physical attributes. Knees had been known to weaken considerably when she turned on the charm and Dan Gallen was no exception to the rule.

"How do you know he can even do these jobs you suggest?" She could tell his heart wasn't in the question. He was merely making a last-ditch effort before caving in.

"He's young, healthy, and strong. What he can't do, he can learn."

"Okay," he said with a deep sigh. "My wife's been wanting some yard work done. Places dug up for flower beds and such. Let me see what she has in mind and I'll get back to you."

Between patients, Jackie talked to many doctors and hospital employees, giving them the same pitch she had given the administrator. Before going to Mark's room, she made a quick trip to a nearby department store and, guessing at his sizes, bought a few things.

"Where did you get this stuff?" he asked suspiciously when she handed him the bag.

"Special hospital fund for such occasions," she replied.

"I'll bet it is. Special Jacqueline Spencer fund, I'll bet."

She made a gesture of indifference. "You can pay me back if it bothers you."

"With what?"

"Haven't you heard? I've been busy. You're now gainfully employed."

"You got me jeans and tennis shoes. I suppose that means you didn't hire me out as assistant surgeon."

When he smiled at her fondly, she wished that he was a good deal less appealing. With that kind of smile, he really didn't need much else to make it through life.

"Next step perhaps. First, however, you'll be raking, mowing, painting, and mulching."

"Marvelous."

"Knocking it?" After all her efforts, she was a little irritated by his sarcastic comment.

He shook his head in dismay. "Lady, I'll never be out of debt to you. But you'll have to excuse my occasional lapses. If you know how I'm going to keep existing, let me know. Where I'll live, how I'll buy food, where I wash these jeans when they're dirty. And *what* I wear while they're washing. God, I hate all this. I can't keep taking and taking from you.".

"Look, Mark," she began softly, "I understand your pride, your confusion, your frustration. You want to apply for welfare benefits?"

"No way," he replied instantly. "I'll mulch, whatever that is."

"I rather supposed you would. But you see, that's what I found out yesterday—you couldn't get welfare benefits if you wanted them. They need information to put on a form before anything can be done."

"Name, rank, and serial number," he said glumly.

"Exactly. And you ain't got none of any."

"Don't remind me."

"Anyway, I told you I'd help and I've done the best I can until you recover or until we manage to locate some relatives or something. I have a few more things to do here. I'll leave while you put on your clothes, then I'll come back and drive you over to Gallen's house. His wife is going to put you to work. Lunch provided, I made sure of that. If you do a good job, you'll get minimum wage, in cash. After I'm done at the office, I'll pick you up there and we'll find a place for you to stay."

"There goes my money already," he quipped. "Exchanging the sweat of my brow for rent."

Mark was strangely silent on the ride to Gallen's house. Assuming he was mildly depressed, and slightly embarrassed over the situation, she did not try to engage him in their usual banter. Perhaps, she thought, it was time to change all that anyway. Obviously he resented the idea of her playing Lady Bountiful. If the resentment continued, the flirtation would stop. And she'd be better off. He grew more appealing by the moment, yet the blankness of his past created a gulf that should not be crossed. But as she drove, glancing occasionally at his strong profile, she already felt the loss. He was no mere object of charity, no yard boy. Mark had class, an innate dignity, and could never be relegated to an inferior position. How I wish, she thought, that he were different. Watching what is happening to him is like witnessing the downfall of a magnificent eagle.

During the day she had little time to check on living quarters for him. What few apartments she did call about were appalling—terrific prices for small, ugly places. At the suggestion of Dr. DePaulo, she called his wife about clothing. Having indulged himself a bit too much the past year or so, he found his closet bulging with garments he could no longer wear. Before going by to pick Mark up that evening, she drove to DePaulo's house and picked up the box his wife had waiting for her.

Mark was still working when she pulled into the Gallens' driveway. Even Jackie, who didn't notice scenery much, could tell the difference in the yard. He smiled and waved when he saw her small car. Rising from the ground, he walked over to her. His new jeans, dark and stiff, were covered with dirt.

"Let me put these tools away," he told her, "and I'll be right with you." He came back quickly, making brushing motions at his jeans as he walked. Running a hand lightly along the fender of her car, he gave a wry smile. "I don't think you'll want me in there."

"No problem," she said casually. "Just hop in and don't worry about it. We can clean out the interior a bit later if necessary."

Mark seemed hesitant, but brushed himself off a little more and then settled himself into the bucket seat. "Nice car," he commented.

"I like it," Jackie replied as she drove them away from the Gallens'. "It's given me no trouble at all and the gas mileage isn't bad. Do you drive?"

He looked at her and gave a small smile, then glanced over at the dash and steering column. "Probably. Want to find out for sure right now?"

"Maybe we should wait till there's less traffic, just in case. Besides, no license."

"This all gets a bit tiresome."

"Looks as if you got a lot done back there," she said.

"I didn't mind it at all," he told her. "After all of those days in the hospital with little or nothing to do, it was good to be occupied. I go back tomorrow. That should finish this one up. By the way, where are we going?"

She flashed him an apologetic look. "To my place." To her own dismay, she blushed under his scrutiny. Kisses exchanged in a hospital corridor were fresh on her mind.

"Dr. Spencer . . ."

"Really, Mark, I haven't had time to look for apartments much. From what I've found out, you can't afford one yet anyway. Not even a rattrap. I have a large place and won't even know you're there. I had a small suite of rooms renovated upstairs for my parents when they visit. You're welcome to use it until you get straightened out. And don't worry about 'charity.' When you see the place, you'll realize there's plenty you can do to earn your rent."

As soon as Jackie pulled the car into her driveway, Mark gave a low whistle. "It's a mansion. I should have expected this, I suppose. You doctors are all rich."

"Not this one," she replied with a laugh. "It's a southern-style mansion all right, but a *small* mansion. When you look closely, you'll see it's badly in need of repair. For years, it was tied up in litigation because so many heirs were involved. No one did anything to keep it up during the whole ordeal. Which is both good and bad. It was a shame to see it crumble, yet if they'd maintained it, I couldn't have afforded it."

She walked with Mark around the house, white frame with many shuttered windows and large columns in the front. "I've had a lot done on the outside—all I could afford so far. But there's still work to be done. And most of the interior is horrid. This place will keep me busy—and broke—for years to come."

"I like it, though. Peaceful and lovely, very gracious. Like its owner." The long, searching look he gave her was warm and personal, but she did her utmost to ignore its meaning.

"And often weary. Would you get that box out of the car and come on in?" She avoided looking directly at him, afraid he could read her mixed emotions too clearly.

By the time Jackie had found the right key and opened the door, Mark was right behind her with the large box. She showed him through the hallway and pointed to a flight of carpeted stairs. "Take it on up. First door on your right. Hope it meets with your approval."

"You mean the box is mine also?"

"Don't get excited, it's just used clothing. A few 'outgrown' things of Dr. DePaulo's. Hope you don't mind. They'll do until you've saved up enough to buy your own. I think the bath is well stocked. If you need anything that isn't there, let me know. Supper will be ready in about an hour."

"Can't I help?" She knew he was standing there with the large box, looking at her expectantly, yet she still managed to avoid eye contact.

"Tonight I'll consider you a guest. After this, you most certainly can."

"We'll have to talk about this situation some more."

This time the tone in his voice compelled her to look at him, and she was struck anew by his devastating attractiveness. Determined to conquer her errant desire, she smiled and said briskly, "Sure, but for right now, go on and clean up."

Curiously content with her decision now that it was made, Jackie freshened up and began preparing a simple evening meal. She even found herself humming a little tune as she worked, something she had not done recently. Jackie had adjusted well to her solitary life. Being a woman who adjusted well to any situation, she had not even realized how solitary her personal life had become. The thought of Mark upstairs getting ready to join her for a meal was pleasant. She did not even pretend to herself at this point that the thought was a purely professional one. Maybe it wasn't wise to have him here, considering the obvious attraction between them. Yet it was only a temporary situation which she could surely control. Wasn't she wise, mature, and strong? Sure she was, she told herself, yet the idea of Mark upstairs caused the blood to flow through her veins a little more quickly, as if it were humming a tune of its own, one over which she had no control.

Chapter Three

❧

Face flushed from the heat given off by the kitchen range, Jackie shoved the rolls into the oven. She had taken one of her frozen casseroles from the freezer and it was almost ready to eat. The tossed green salad was waiting, crisp and cold, in the refrigerator. Once in a while, on a day off, Jackie would go on a cooking binge and spend hours in the kitchen. She would cook large amounts of several recipes, then divide them into aluminum containers for freezing. This made it easy for her to have a good, nutritious meal when she was too tired—or too lazy—to cook.

When she moved away from the oven, she saw Mark watching her from the doorway. He looked scrubbed and vitally sexy. His skin had taken on color from his day in the sun and his very dark hair curled damply at his forehead. Fresh from the shower, he did more for that blue polo shirt than pudgy Dr. DePaulo had ever done. On DePaulo, a "Large" had accommodated flab; on Mark, it accommodated an impressive breadth of firm male musculature. Again waves of doubts assailed her. Ignoring this vital maleness was increasingly difficult.

She gave him a faint smile to acknowledge his presence.

He did not move into the kitchen itself but remained in the doorway, filling it almost completely. With a languor approaching insolence, his eyes appraised her, not missing a thing. Her navy-colored slacks were formfitting and her white, navy, and lime-green blouse was open at the throat, its colors and thin fabric appearing cool and summery. Self-consciously she pushed back a strand of her dark hair that, in the heat and hurry, had fallen carelessly out of place.

"I've not seen you like this before," he commented. In her opinion, his eyes dwelt overlong on the rise and fall of her breasts against the light, clinging blouse she wore, and he was a bit too openly appreciative of her trim, yet femininely rounded, hips.

"I'm wearing what I had on all day," she said as casually as possible.

"Minus that omnipresent white coat," he pointed out. "A coat like that can hide a multitude of sins. In your case, the sin comes in covering up."

"Hmmm. How about cutting the flattery and helping?"

"I thought you said I was a guest tonight."

"I've just changed my mind. As I'm sure you've already noticed, this mausoleum isn't air-conditioned, and I've already heated the kitchen up with the oven. Would you mind setting the table out on the patio? I think it will be much cooler out there."

After Mark had completed the assigned task, he returned to help Jackie carry the meal out. "One of these days I'll modernize this kitchen," she told him. "The last time anyone did anything in here must have been about World War II."

The kitchen was huge. It was also ugly. The high ceiling and walls were painted a stark white and the cabinets were white metal. They tended to rattle ominously when one walked across the linoleum-covered floor. The tan linoleum, atrocious when new, had certainly not improved with age. To serve the dual purpose of covering up the bare spots and making the atmosphere more cheerful, Jackie had added brightly colored throw rugs here and there. They didn't help a lot.

"I see this room with brick walls, a fireplace, lots of natural wood, and plenty of brass accents."

"Me, too," she agreed, giving him a wry smile. "But you're 'seeing' thousands of dollars. Eventually, though, I'll get it done."

"I'm beginning to see what you mean about keeping busy and broke the rest of your life. Although I shouldn't think it would be a problem for a doctor. The money, I mean."

"I'm not a rich, society doctor, Mark. I'm just a doctor doctor. Most of my patients are too poor to have savings or good insurance and too well off to have welfare benefits. A lot of the time my payment consists of a bright smile and a thank-you."

"I have a feeling this is the choice you've made, doctor." His expression was somewhat mocking.

"Very perceptive of you. And by the way, you don't have to keep calling me 'doctor.' Makes me feel old and frumpish."

"You know you're neither."

She shrugged and did not pursue that line of conversation. "I know I could start a practice in a more prestigious area, but I like feeling needed. But give me a little credit. I know what I am and don't even pretend I'm 'noble.' I'm selfish enough to revel in the glory of being needed."

"No apologies necessary."

"I didn't mean it as an apology."

"Explanation, then," Mark said. "Needing you myself, I happen to think your goals and ambitions are great."

Under the scrutiny of his keen eyes, Jackie grew even more uncomfortable. She knew he was not speaking of his medical need as a patient but of his more primitive need as a man and she also knew he meant her to understand his intent. Warning sirens went off inside her mind once more, saying, "Jackie, keep away from this man, at least until you know if he's free and that his past holds no serious barriers."

She pulled the conversation back to the house, to the safe subject of architecture and interior decorating. Just as they were finishing up their meal the telephone rang. When Jackie returned to the patio, her glum face caused Mark to say, "Emergency call?"

"Not quite that bad. My friend Marge is coming over." Catching his eye, she laughed and explained, "Marge is a good friend and I love her dearly. We went through high school together and started college together. When I branched off to premed and she branched off to prewife, we still kept in close contact. She lives only a few minutes from here, and it's her goal in life to get me married off so I'll have just as much to complain about as she does. *After* she gets here and we've talked, I'll enjoy her company and be glad she dropped by. I know it must sound awful, but I *am* tired and was looking forward to relaxing and reading."

"Something light like the annals of neurology?"

"After all, I have to keep up," she replied with a teasing smile. "Although I do manage to sneak in a novel here and there. Especially a good mystery or detective story. I just sit back and enjoy them, don't even try to find out who 'dunnit.' But don't knock the annals of neurology. It's a fascinating subject."

"Do tell." Again he seemed to mock her, but not in an ugly way. Really, almost affectionately.

"Think about it, Mark," she insisted. "Look at your own case. You can't remember a thing about your past, not even your real name. Yet you can remember all the words you ever knew, can talk and converse without a hitch."

They talked for a while longer, the shadows changing as the sun went down. It was almost completely dark when they got up to do the dishes. As was her habit, Marge knocked at the back door, then walked on in. Her short, blond friend's eyes grew wide at the sight of Mark. "Gosh, Jackie, you should have told me you already had company. I don't want to interrupt anything."

"You're not," Jackie reassured.

"A regrettable fact," Mark commented, grinning for Marge's benefit.

"Mark, this is my good friend, Marge McPherson. Marge, this is Mark Dolan. He's a patient—and a new friend."

After Marge and Mark had exchanged pleasantries, Mark said, "If you'll excuse me, ladies, I'll let you visit with each other."

"You don't need to leave on my account," Marge protested.

"I'm not. I hate to admit it, but today was a bit of a strain for me."

"I suppose you saw the TV and stereo in your rooms, Mark. If you want a book to read, check my study. It's down the hall a way, on your right. It's one of the few nice rooms. The decor is practically wall-to-wall books.

"Thanks," he said and walked off.

During Jackie's last comments, Marge's eyes kept growing wider. When at last Jackie turned to look at her, she saw her friend was nearly bursting with suppressed curiosity and excitement.

"Come on into the other room," Jackie invited, "and then ask your questions, dear Margaret, before your eyes fall completely out of your head."

"He's staying *here*?" Marge asked, not waiting until she was seated in the comfortable but shabby chair. "When he said he'd leave and let us visit, I assumed he meant he was going home . . . then *you* said . . ."

"I know what he said and what I said. After all, I was there."

"You're dragging this out on purpose," Marge accused, "just because you know I'm about to die of curiosity."

"Could be," Jackie admitted playfully.

"Then quit. It isn't nice."

"Well, he's a patient who doesn't have a home. Or, that is, I suppose he has one, he just doesn't know where it is."

"And so he's staying here, just like that?"

"That's it."

Marge shook her head in disbelief. "You have to be insane, kid."

"I've brought home patients before. For short periods."

"Uh-huh. Troubled kids and young girls, displaced elderly people, but not a hunk like that. God, he's cute. A man like that is enough to make a woman give up marriage."

Jackie laughed at her bubbly friend. "You know you wouldn't give up Rich for anything or anyone."

"True," Marge replied with a sigh, "but we all have

moments of temptation. Anyway, back to the serious side of it. You *can't* let that man stay here."

"Why not?" Jackie soon wished she had not asked this question, for Marge launched herself into a lengthy dissertation on the possibility of rape, murder, theft, and "what people will say." After listening calmly and without comment, Jackie then told Marge the story of Mark's amnesia and the technical difficulties they had experienced in obtaining help for him.

"I understand why you're doing it," Marge said. "You always were a softy. But, still, this time . . . I mean, surely you can see why you can't."

Tactfully, Jackie steered the conversation around to Marge herself and her unending problems with Rich, her three children, and her part-time job as a buyer for a chain store. Perhaps, she thought, she should confide her attraction to Mark to Marge, but she did not. It was a difficult thing to put into words.

After they had chatted a long time, Jackie stretched and yawned. Marge glanced at the clock. "Gracious, I better get home. Rich'll be wondering if I dropped off in a hole somewhere. The weight I'm gaining, though, it'd have to be a big hole." She patted her slightly protruding stomach ruefully as she got up. On the way out the door, she said rather loudly, "Don't be a stubborn fool, Jackie. For once in your life, listen to someone else."

"He's no murderer or rapist, Marge," she said impatiently. "I'm perceptive enough to know that."

"There's still a great deal of potential danger there. And if *my* perception is correct, the greatest danger is involvement. You know nothing of that man. Nothing at all."

"Good night, Marge," she said firmly.

She closed and locked the door, then turned to find that Mark had reentered the kitchen. The sober look he wore told her he had overheard Marge's parting words.

"Came to get a drink," he said.

Jackie smiled when she saw the soft drink can in his hand. "I think I know something else about you," she said.

"Something good?"

"Definitely. You aren't a drug or alcohol addict. All these days without any signs of withdrawal or any desire expressed for a drink."

"Maybe I just forgot that, too."

She shook her head, choosing to answer him in a serious vein. "Your mind might have forgotten, but your body couldn't. Any serious problem would have made itself known by now."

On a moment's whim, Jackie unlocked the door she had just locked and stepped outside. Mark followed her. "Since you've worked in a yard all day, you might be interested in seeing this one. Once upon a time, it was a place of regal beauty. When I bought it, it was a tangled wilderness. Now, I suppose, it's somewhere between the extremes of wilderness and garden."

Although the hour was quite late, the backyard was bathed softly in the pale light of a full moon. The ancient trees rose to meet the sky, then graciously let their branches drape over the lawn. Strands of Spanish moss added, at night, an eerie aspect to the atmosphere. As they made their way through the yard a piece of the hanging moss caught in Mark's hair and he brushed it away. "Still a bit of a wilderness," he commented.

"You wouldn't say that if you'd seen it before. Everything is relative. See, I even planted some flowers early this spring."

She bent toward the shallow beds filled with easy-to-grow annuals such as marigolds and petunias. They appeared more delicate in the soft moonlight, the colors muted.

"What does a woman like you—a woman alone, that is—want with a huge old house like this? Isn't it more trouble than it's worth?"

"You wouldn't believe the number of times I've been asked that. But when I was a child, I dreamed of living in a restored house of this style, all white-columned graciousness. Admittedly, when I first bought it a few years ago, I had visions of filling it with a family. Even now, when I don't expect that will happen, I don't regret buying it. It's my home and I love it."

"I can see that. And it is well on its way to becoming a place of beauty. Undoubtedly you could sell it at a handsome profit."

"Maybe you're a hard-boiled businessman," she observed. "No room for sentimentality or whim."

Maintaining a companionable silence, they walked back toward the house. The light from the big kitchen window threw out a welcoming beacon.

"Your friend is right, you know," Mark said when they were near the door.

"Sorry you had to hear all that. Marge lets her imagination get carried away at times."

"Not this time. She's right. You've done a foolish thing, a dangerous thing."

"I don't fear you, Mark."

"Then perhaps you should, Jacqueline Marie." When he caught her by the arms and pulled her against him, she did not protest. Later she could not have said if the yielding had to do with surprise or with the desire for his touch that had been building within her. When his mouth closed upon hers, she wanted to kiss him back and did so. Sensing her compliance, he dropped his hold on her arms and enfolded her, cradling her against him. Their long kiss was warm and tender, in tune with the moonlight and scent of lilacs.

He pulled his face away from hers, looking at her with eyes that spoke of gentle desire. Unable and unwilling to stop herself, she put her arms around him, letting her fingers entwine themselves in the longish hair at the back of his neck. When he bent to kiss her again, she was as ready and eager as he was. Their mouths pressed together, parted, explored, and Jackie was filled with a mellow helplessness. With a will of its own, her body pressed its softness against him, wanting to melt and merge with his glorious, taut maleness. "Jackie," he murmured. She cut off further comment by offering her lips again, parting them quickly to accept his fiery, probing tongue.

She let her hands roam freely across his broad back, delighting in its firmness and strength. Shivering slightly when he dropped butterfly kisses along her neck and on her eyelids, she eagerly welcomed the return of his mouth to hers. Forms pressed together, they continued to cling and kiss, desire that was both sweet and wild mounting until all reason was lost in total sensuality. Her mouth was bruised and swollen, yet she protested if he moved away and pulled his head back down to meet hers.

Aching with a need such as she had never before experienced, she was beyond any hope of self-control. When, suddenly, he let her go and stepped back, she felt an almost violent reaction. Moaning his name, she reached out for him. But instead of embracing her, he caught her wrist with his left hand and, with his right hand, held her chin. The kiss he gave her then spoke of tenderness. And of farewell.

"Mark . . ." she said again, feeling she would surely perish if he did not hold her once more.

"We can't, Jackie, love. You know that."

"Mark, I . . ." Her eyes were deep with hurt and unfulfilled hunger as they searched his face.

"Don't. We both fully realize the danger now. There are too many complications for us to allow this to happen."

"And if we can't help it?" A slight bitterness was beginning to replace raging desire.

"Oh, we can help it, honey. I won't let this happen again. I happen to think way too much of you to do anything that might hurt you. I could be anything or anyone—married, in trouble, who knows? It's a rotten deal for both of us. Because I want to make love to you. Oh, my sweet, I do. So bad it hurts." He lifted her wrist to his lips and kissed the soft, vulnerable flesh over her pulse point. This caused the blood within those veins to flow hotly, rapidly.

"Mark, kiss me one more time. Please, just once more."

His face was a tortured mask but he did not respond to her request. "No, darling, no more. If we ever start again, we won't stop where we did tonight. It's going to take more than kisses in the moonlight to assuage what we feel. And I can't let that happen to you."

He walked away and Jackie forced herself to suppress the impulse to run after him, to beg him to make love to her regardless of the consequences. After a few solitary moments in the garden, she walked slowly back to the house, locked the door once more, went up to her room and undressed. While the bathwater was running, she looked objectively at her unclothed self in the full-length mirror. She had a body made for love, for love *tonight* with Mark, that intriguing stranger at the other end of the hall. Knowing she had to deny this body of hers, she seethed at her insanity in having brought him here. The sexual tension between them, the kiss that occurred when he was still in the hospital . . . She had thought she was strong enough to ignore it, to do battle against it.

Well, she resolved, despite those moments of weakening, she would be strong. She had no other choice. As long as memory of the past eluded Mark, the situation was too risky. Any damage she suffered right now was minor compared to the heartache that could occur if she gave in to loving him fully, then lost him when the clouds had cleared from his past.

Drawn by the scent of bacon and eggs, Mark came to the kitchen the next morning. Although Jackie was very aware of his presence, she did not turn to look at him. A long, very modest robe covered her form completely.

"Morning," he said.

"Hi," she replied with false brightness, still not daring to look his way.

True to his word, he kept both a psychological and a physical distance from her. No mention was made of the previous evening as they discussed plans for the day and their transportation arrangements. He offered to clear the kitchen while she dressed for work, and she accepted that offer.

When she returned to the kitchen, he was having a last cup of coffee. He looked up at her and smiled. Seeing that sensual mouth curving in a smile, it was impossible not to remember the way it had felt against hers. Seeming to read her thoughts, he said, "Want to talk about it?"

She hesitated for a moment, then shrugged. "I don't know what there is to talk about. I suppose I find it embarrassing that you had to have the control."

"It wasn't easy," he said gently.

She gave a deep sigh. "Believe me, Mark, I know all the arguments against getting involved with you. I've mulled them over in my mind since I met you. One, it's not professional. Two, you are still, in a sense, 'ill.' Three, I know nothing of your past; it's very probable you have commitments elsewhere. Four, even without commitments, your past could hold obstacles for us. Five, you need to be thinking clearly before you enter a new relationship; right now what you're feeling toward me may be as much gratitude as anything else; that's commonplace in a patient-doctor situation. Six . . ."

"Hey," he protested with a laugh. "That's enough for now. And you're right enough about all of it, except for one thing—although I *am* grateful for your medical attention, gratitude has little to do with my feelings for you. But more than desire, I care for you. Care too much to risk hurting you if my past turns out to be murky or 'involved.' "

"Thank you," she said, her words sounding slightly choked. Her arguments all did make sense. The fact that Mark agreed with her should make it easier. Somehow it did not. His gallant desire to protect her only drew her to him all the more.

At the hospital, she got caught up in the ceaseless round of activities and managed to edge thoughts of Mark out of her mind somewhat, though not entirely. By having him in her house, she had created a situation in which it would be all too easy to lose control again. She made a mental note to check on apartments again. Moving him to his own place would be the best for both of them.

Her thoughts were interrupted when Dr. Hamilton called to her from the end of the hospital corridor. "Jackie, just thought you might want to know a trace of amphetamines was found in Amy's blood. Lucky for us we had a specimen drawn before she was here much longer."

Jackie gave a pleased smile. "I just felt it *had* to be something like that. Her seizures didn't seem typical epileptiform to me. How was she getting the stuff?"

"Neighbor kid. Something he found in a big brother's dresser drawer. Rotten kid apparently knew it was 'dope' of some sort and got curious. Wanted to see what it did but was too scared to take it himself. So he was feeding it to Amy, making a show of playing doctor and telling her they were candy pills."

"I'm so glad the problem's been solved. The child should be all right once it all gets out of her system."

"Yeah, and thanks for your help. Sorry about my dubious attitude."

"Forget it. Happens to us all."

Before Jackie got out of the hospital, she ended up promising Dr. Jeff Pitillo that she would take his turn in ER that night. Although he told her he would take her turn the next week, she doubted that he would. His intentions were good, yet something always seemed to come up.

At her office, Marge called and asked her for dinner that night. Jackie pleaded off because of the ER duty but said she could come the next night.

"Uh, Jackie," Marge said, "if that man's still at your house, bring him along."

"You just want to get Rich's opinion of him," Jackie accused, making a face at the receiver.

"Could be, but he's still welcome to come. And I'll be civil."

"Hmmm. I'll see."

When Jackie picked Mark up that evening, she handed him the car keys. He looked at them rather blankly. "You're going to have to try driving," she said. "Pull in and out of the driveway here. If you make that, then go around the block a few times till you get the feel of it."

"What's up?" he asked.

"I have to go back for ER duty. I only ran out long enough to pick you up because you didn't have a ride home. You need to drop me off at the hospital. Very soon."

He shrugged and got in the silver and blue car, adjusting the seat to accommodate his long legs. "Okay, now we know I can drive," he commented after the second time around the block. "Only, under the present circumstances, I can't get a driver's license."

"Then you'll just have to drive without one," she replied. "You can use that little pickup truck in the garage. Just be extremely careful, or we'll both get in trouble."

His hands gripped the steering wheel so tightly his knuckles showed white. "Jackie, I can't keep accepting and accepting from you. We're going to have to do something else."

"We will. In fact, I made a note to check on apartments tomorrow, though they won't solve the car problem." Then, to change the subject, she told him of the invitation to Marge's house. He expressed some reluctance, suspicious that he would be subjected to scrutiny. But using the argument that a new environment might jar some memories, Jackie persuaded him to go.

By the time she got home, it was very late. Although a light burned and a note on the refrigerator indicated she had a plate left in the warming oven, Mark had not waited up.

She didn't know if she was glad or sorry, then decided it didn't matter. Being so tired, she doubted if anything or anyone could keep her awake. When she did go to sleep, however, her last thought was of Mark Dolan and of the way she had felt within his embrace.

On the way to the McPhersons' the next evening, Jackie turned to Mark and, with a wry smile, said, "You do great things for DePaulo's clothes." In the light-colored blazer and sport shirt, Mark looked nothing less than fantastic. After several days of outside work, his skin was tanned a golden brown and he had cut his hair recently.

If she hadn't known better, she would have guessed him to be someone wealthy and polished. He looked *that* good. To the manor born, really, she thought wryly. But, then, for all she knew—or he knew—he *was* to the manor born.

That's it, kid, she thought, keep reminding yourself how anonymous he is. Constant reminders seemed to be necessarily. If anyone had ever possessed a presence and virility that defied anonymity, it was this man standing before her now.

"Thanks," he said, his dark eyes flicking across her with obvious appreciation. In keeping with his resolution not to break the impersonal barrier they maintained, he gave her no flowerly compliments. She had enough feminine vanity, however, to know she looked good in the white cotton sundress, simply cut, with tall ankle-strapped sandals that displayed her legs to a nice advantage. Her mahogany-colored hair was brushed to a high gloss, each side pulled back slightly and caught up with a barrette in the back.

The dinner at the McPhersons' house went with less strain than she had anticipated. No one scrutinized Mark openly and he was not subjected to a barrage of questions. Even curious Marge restrained herself from making sly comments and innuendos. Although they had been fed their meal earlier, the three small McPhersons kept popping in and out. Even if the atmosphere was casual, Marge did have an appreciation for fine things. The meal was served with the best of linen, silver, crystal, and china.

Throughout dinner, Jackie observed Mark closely, though surreptitiously. He was relaxed and easy with the children and did not seem to be uncomfortable with the assortment of eating utensils. From time to time, however, he would pause and look at things very carefully. At those moments, an odd expression crossed his face. He's remembering something, Jackie thought; I'm sure he's remembering something. She did not feel as elated at the idea as she thought she would be.

When the McPherson boys were at last persuaded to go to bed, they shook hands with Mark manfully. Little Sarah, however, threw herself into his arms and gave him a big hug and kiss just like the ones she had given her parents and Jackie. Mark watched them thoughtfully as they paraded reluctantly out of the room. He was very quiet for a few moments before he let himself be drawn back into the conversation.

"I'm not sure where I'll go from here," Mark told Rich and Marge. "My doctor here advised me that three months is the magic time period. What I don't remember by then, I probably won't. If, by that time, I don't remember anything and no one has stepped forward to 'claim me,' I suppose I'll have to go through some legal procedure to establish a new identity. Then I'll have to see about some educational training of some sort. I don't think I'm cut out to be a gardener and carpenter." He held out his calloused and scraped hands with a rueful smile.

Jackie was pleased at his frank and open discussion of his predicament. Knowing the McPhersons were curious but too polite to probe, he told them what they wanted to know with ease.

"It's a weird situation, Dolan," Rich commented once, obviously fascinated by Mark's story.

"You're telling me? Sometimes I can't believe this is happening."

Soon the conversation moved to books, then movies, and finally to current events. Marge served a light after-dinner wine, pouring it into goblets as thin and fine as any ever crafted. Mark held his out in front of him, once touching the delicate rim and regarding it solemnly through narrowed eyes.

It was quite late when they left for home. Jackie tossed the keys at Mark. "Would you mind driving? Suddenly I'm tired and just want to relax."

"Okay, but I'm still not happy about this driving I'm doing. It *is* illegal, you know."

"I know, but you're probably a licensed driver anyway."

"Just see what a nice policeman has to say about that," he warned cynically.

"No sweat," Jackie replied airily. "I'm a doctor and you're escorting me to an emergency call. They oughta buy that."

He maneuvered the car skillfully down the street. From the corner of his eye, he cast her a reproachful glance. "That wouldn't be honest, doctor, now would it?"

She gave a little giggle. "Then I suppose I'll just have to rely on my feminine charm if and when you're stopped."

"That would work better anyway. No one would believe you're a doctor. Not the way you look in that dress."

"And how do I look in this dress?" Perhaps she should feel sorry that his resolve was melting and that he was responding to her femininity, but she didn't.

"Fishing for a compliment?"

"Of course."

"You look like . . . well, like an exquisite magnolia blossom. A veritable southern belle." She giggled again, then tucked her legs into the bucket seat beneath her. Mark shot her a look of amusement. "You're in a different mood tonight. Too much wine?"

"No," she denied. "I think it's just the effect of a relaxed evening. I've worked awfully long hours this week. Forgive me a little silliness?"

"I'd forgive you anything, Jacqueline. Anything at all."

"You remembered something tonight, didn't you, Mark?"

"You're very astute."

"We southern belles can fool you. Are you going to tell me what it is?"

"Of course. I was just still sorting it out in my mind,

trying to make some sense of it. I saw myself in those kids, recalled a few memories from childhood. Maybe they aren't even memories, just feelings, moods. And all that opulent silver and crystal. It was so familiar. I think I must have been wealthy, Jackie. Or at least I was around nice things in some way."

"Great. When you get it all worked out, let me know. I may be able to collect a big fee on this one yet."

"Whatever you choose to charge, I'll find a way to pay it, even if it costs my very life."

"How noble and poetic."

"Ain't it, though? As memories go, I guess that's a poor start."

"No, Mark, really, it's fantastic. Anything at all is encouraging. And it could be like the beginning of an avalanche. Once it starts sliding, there'll be no stopping it."

He pulled into the garage, then opened the car door for her and the door to the house. Both times, his hand grazed against hers, lightly and accidentally. Both times she was seized with a longing that knew no bounds.

As his physician, she was pleased with his progress. As a woman, who despite all resolve was falling in love with him, she felt a strange fear. It was highly likely that his return to full memory, or even a partial return that restored his identity, would take him away from her. He was not from Mississippi. He was not hers. Trying to accept that fact was becoming increasingly difficult.

As they told each other good night and parted circumspectly, his eyes caught hers once, then dropped away almost immediately. The desire was still between them, waiting, hoping, doing its silent battle with prudence.

Jackie hoped Mark's memory was restored before desire won out over prudence. But she didn't hope it as hard as she felt she should have. The times when she was gripped with an urge to seize each moment as it happened, to ignore the fears about Mark's past, to let the future take care of itself, were occurring more frequently. It would appear that her worst enemies in this battle were her own emotions. She was a woman who was accustomed to self-discipline, but now she had to constantly remind herself to be on guard.

Chapter Four

The next day, Sunday, was an odd one, both externally and internally. The weather was muggy. No breeze stirred and no comfort was to be found. A scant few moments after showering and putting on fresh clothing, Jackie felt hot and irritable. Inside the house she felt in danger of suffocating from the closeness. Outside the heat was slightly less oppressive but there one had to contend with the merciless mosquitoes.

She understood her own odd reaction to the slight improvement in Mark's memory, understood even if she did not approve. She knew she should be pleased for him, and her discomfort with her own reaction only added to the general misery of the day. Strangely enough, Mark did not seem in a very good mood himself.

He slept late, then did some yard work and inside repairs on the house, but he seemed unusually clumsy, and his work was frequently interrupted as he spilled, dropped, and broke things, and inflicted bodily injury on himself. She heard him muttering fiercely to himself on several occasions and felt it was probably just as well that she could not hear his comments. When she offered to fix him lunch, he curtly refused and continued to drink glass after glass of ice water and ice tea. Not being hungry herself, Jackie did not press the matter. She settled for some melon, then changed into a swimsuit. She thought the bright blue one-piece was rather modest. While she reclined with a book on a beach towel in the yard, Mark passed by and glared at her.

"What are you so grumpy about?" she asked him, aware that she sounded none too pleasant herself. The constant awareness of Mark's presence, the constant need to be on guard . . . it had her nerves pulled taut.

"You don't make it easy, Jacqueline. You test a man beyond endurance."

"You mean this suit? What do you want me to wear when the temperature and humidity are both nearly one hundred? A down jacket?"

"Forget it."

"That's what I plan on doing."

"May I use the truck to go somewhere? I'll buy the gas, of course."

"You don't need to ask. Use the truck or car, whichever you want." She was dying to ask where he was going, but could not.

"I just have to get out of here, Jackie. This isn't working. I'll have to come up with something else." He turned on his heels and was gone with the quiet grace of a big cat.

The heat intensified as the afternoon passed. A nurse at St. John's called and said one of her patients had gotten worse. Although Jackie did not, of course, want any harm to come to Helen Nichols, she was almost grateful for the excuse to go to the hospital. It was, at least, air-conditioned. Once there, she took her time and visited with several hospital employees.

"We'll be lucky if we don't have a storm before the

day's over," was a frequently heard comment. Jackie tended to agree with the weather forecast. She had lived in Mississippi all her life and knew these unbearable summer days often ended with a cooling, though frightening, thunderstorm.

After rounds, Jackie went to visit the patients in the geriatric ward, people who seldom had visitors and were grateful for anyone who would talk to them for a while. She did not feel in the least noble about her visit, confessing to herself that she was doing it rather than going home to the almost unbearable sexual tension between herself and Mark. She cheered the elderly patients and they cheered her, but when she left them there were still many hours remaining in the long day.

This is ridiculous, she told herself, not wanting to go home when she had always enjoyed her home so much. She turned the little car's air conditioner on full blast and headed home. She knew it was the last cold air she was likely to feel that day, unless she went out. She considered dinner and a movie, then rejected the idea. Nothing appealed to her.

Ron Piper, a young man she had dated from time to time, called and invited her to an impromptu swimming party and picnic one of his neighbor's was forming. She knew she should go, but she responded with a polite excuse that sounded like a polite excuse.

Her lack of appetite persisted but she forced herself to eat a light evening meal. She did a load of laundry, straightened up the house a bit, worked on a crossword puzzle, read a medical journal, and then hunted through the garage until she found a small can of white paint. With halfhearted strokes, she gave a new coat of paint to the lawn furniture. None of these endeavors granted her any peace of mind. Due to the continued heat and to the excess of white paint on her hands and legs, she took her third shower of the day. Hoping for a cooling effect, she sprinkled her body liberally with baby powder and slipped on a white cotton nightshirt.

Ten o'clock and the heat had not broken at all. And Mark had not come home. Where had he gone, she wondered. She shouldn't care, and yet she did. If he had left the house because he was tormented by desire, then she preferred not to know where he was. A man like that, so magnetic and personable, would have no trouble finding a willing partner. The thought of Mark with another woman caused a pain that was almost physical.

Only stubbornness kept her from taking a sedative so that she could relax and sleep. Her one concession to her unsettled emotional state was to take two aspirin tablets and drink a glass of milk. For a long time, she was acutely aware of each car that passed along her street. Gradually she stopped expecting him to come home. She became almost lulled by the sound of each engine, the flash of each pair of headlights. Eventually she fell into a sleep that was deep, yet still uneasy.

The sound of the storm did not awaken her. The dampness did. Springing from her bed, she ran to the window and closed it. Rain was coming down in torrents, blown in sheets by an angry wind. The thunder roared, and seconds later, the darkness was rent by a wild, yellow light. She ran madly from room to room, closing all the windows. The rain that blew in through the windows as she shut them soaked her hair and gown. She found rags and mopped most of the water from the windowsills, fearing the wetness would damage the old wood. Wet and weary, she did what she could and turned to go back to bed when Mark suddenly burst into the kitchen looking almost as wet as Jackie was. All he had on was a pair of white tennis shorts.

"My gosh, a fellow could drown out there," he said, water dripping in puddles about him on the worn linoleum.

"Look what you're doing to my clean floor," she pointed out, sounding and feeling unreasonable under the circumstances.

"And what do you think you're doing to it yourself, doctor?" he countered.

Jackie looked down at the puddle surrounding her, left by the drenched and dripping hem of her nightshirt. She laughed then. "Oh, it feels so much better, such a relief. A refreshing end to a miserable day."

Mark did not reply. His eyes, their expression somehow smoky, moved across her form, and she suddenly realized the wet, white fabric of her nightshirt must be diaphanous.

"We both look a mess. Here, catch." She threw him a towel, then began rubbing at her own shoulder-length hair with another one. Although she attempted lightness, she was aware of the shakiness of her voice. "Where were you when it came up?" she asked. "It took me by surprise. Usually a storm wakes me, but the water was coming through the windows in buckets before I knew anything about it."

He gave her a look she could not accurately interpret. "I was here. I've been here for ages."

"Oh. I didn't hear you come in."

"Didn't know I was supposed to report."

"Don't be an idiot. Of course you're not supposed to report. How did you get so wet, then?"

"Went outside to rescue your flowerpots in those hanging baskets. They were blowing about like crazy."

"Thanks. I appreciate it."

"It's nothing."

"Need a dry towel?"

He moved his broad shoulders in a gesture of indifference. Wetness still gleamed across his chest, matting the black, curling hair. "I guess I'll go on up to bed anyway. Anything else you need me to do first?"

What a loaded question, she thought wryly. Her spoken response, however, was civil and appropriate. "No, everything's fine. Sleep well. On second thought, though . . . I didn't go in your room. You'll need to close the window, so would you mind sponging up the water? And maybe you should unplug your TV set. The lightning is terrible."

As if to prove her point, a sudden flash lit up the kitchen more brightly than any fluorescent bulb could do.

"Yes, ma'am," he replied mockingly and turned to go.

"Mark, where did you go tonight?" The question escaped against her will. She felt the painful blush of embarrassment steal up her neck and across her face, and was grateful for the darkness. Before he could reply, she said quickly, "Forget I asked that. I shouldn't have. You have my apologies."

"No apologies necessary. Call if you need anything, Jackie. Or don't storms frighten you?"

"Not really. Like other things I can't prevent, I just accept them as they are and enjoy what I can."

Mark turned without comment and went up to his room. Jackie cleaned up a few more puddles and climbed the carpeted stairs. Just as she was going into her room, there was a ferocious burst of thunder and a bolt of lightning that seemed to split the sky apart. The few lights she had left burning went out, and an unfamiliar silence descended upon the house.

"You okay, Jackie?" Mark asked, emerging from his rooms.

"I'm okay—just startled. I have some candles and matches in my room. Let me get you some."

She entered her room, strange now in its darkness, and groped her way over to the dresser where she felt about in one of the top drawers until she found the squat, sturdy candles and the box of matches. Lighting two candles, she placed one on the dresser and carried the other to Mark. He had not come into her room but stood politely in the hall.

She held out the candle. When he took it, his hands enfolded hers momentarily, and something glowed between them with more heat and intensity than the candle flame radiated. To her dismay, tears sprang to her eyes. She released her fingers from the candle and turned away, but too late.

"Jackie, what's the matter?"

"Nothing. Nothing at all. Everything is peachy keen."

"Don't be sarcastic. It doesn't become you."

The tears evaporated and she turned to face him, her eyes still shining from the recent moisture. "Then what does become me, Mark?"

"Patience. Sweetness. Strength."

"And when I'm tired of being all that? When I can't be strong anymore, what then?"

"I want to hold you. Comfort you."

"Then why don't you?"

"Jackie, darling, you know why I don't."

Her back was against the wall on one side of the hall, and Mark's back was against the opposite wall. He continued to hold the chubby candle, its dim light emphasizing the shadows on his strong features. Her high, proud breasts, the suppleness of her entire body, were clearly visible through the wet gown. She did not care. If he wanted her, so be it. This terrible hunger was not to be borne alone. In the background, the rain kept on descending in great, swooping sheets punctuated by thunder and lightning. Several feet away from him, she felt her body sway involuntarily, wanting to be closer, wanting to be held and caressed.

"I went through hell tonight, thinking you'd gone to be with someone else." Pride no longer mattered.

"I've gone through hell the past several nights, just knowing you were here in the same house with me. But it can't be, Jackie."

She moved a few steps toward him. Bodies still apart, she traced his jawline with her finger, then ran the finger across his mouth. The intake of his breath was sharp, audible. "I could be a bad person, hon. A criminal. Anything."

"That isn't likely. You're clearly too highbrow."

"Even members of the Mafia get educated and cultured," he warned.

"Tell me about it." They still did not touch but a shadow could not have passed between them. Her body felt as hot as the candle flame. She would not have been surprised to see it cast a glow.

"The real danger is that I'm committed elsewhere. The last thing I want to do is to hurt you."

"I know all that, Mark."

And she did. But the wise, mature, sensible lady-physician was gone. Jackie was a woman in love, and all-consuming desire was not to be denied. She took the candle from him and he released it without protest. Taking his hand, she led him down the hall toward her room. She pushed open the door and blew out Mark's candle. Her own wide, spacious bed chamber was eerily, dimly lit from the one candle on the dresser top.

"There's a limit to how strong I can be." His voice was thick, nearly hoarse.

"I love you, Mark. Right now you're mine. Maybe tomorrow, or the next day, when your memory comes back, we'll find you can't be mine. So *now* will have to be enough. We have to live for now, for tonight. The future isn't something we can control."

"Jackie, love. You're sure?"

"I'm sure."

He placed a hand in the thick dampness of her hair, fingers tangling in the mass of it. For a brief moment, his eyes burned into hers, then closed, and he pressed his lips to hers. Giving a shudder close to ecstasy, Jackie pushed herself against him. His impatient hands freed her from the damp, clinging garment, then touched the fullness of her pretty breasts for the first time. Knees too weak to stand any longer, she moved toward the bed, and he moved with her fluidly, easily. He helped her lie down, his eyes dark and burning as they surveyed her body in repose. Within a moment, he was also fully unclothed and lying beside her, his lean, muscular body magnificently beautiful.

Without clothing, they were equal and unafraid. His past did not matter, nor did anything else about him, except the fact that he was here with her now, loving and loved. When they kissed, the contours of their bodies molded together as if they were meant to be like this, now and forever. She pulled his head against her bosom, and when his mouth worked its magic on her soft flesh, she cried aloud, laughing at the sheer joy and pleasure of his unrestricted touch. Growing more bold, his hands sought out the most vulnerable and secret places of her being. Wanton, longing, she encouraged his deepening caresses, firing Mark's desire with petal-soft movements of her fingertips.

"Please, oh, yes, please now," she murmured feverishly, unable to sustain the blissful tension any longer. Neither of them had any thought of control left. Mark's passion met hers, matched it, surpassed it. Overwhelmed by the sheer masculine power of him, she let herself be carried along the path of all-consuming lovemaking. The surging hunger of their bodies, the cries that escaped them at the height of ecstasy, the crash of thunder and jagged streaks of lightning, the sound of heavy rain against the room and the trees—all these things and more combined inseparably, until the sounds and movements of the storm were indistinguishable from the sounds and movements of their shared sensuality. Now, in this moment, all her fears seemed foolish. This love they shared was too great to be ignored. They had to live for the here and now, and they moved, crested, and subsided in perfect cadence with the storm.

When it was over for them, they lay silently, slightly apart, reacting as if they were stunned. Jackie's breathing remained heavy and the rising and falling of her chest was rapid. While she had wanted Mark and had expected it to be good with them, she had not been fully prepared for the cascade of glory she had just experienced. Daring at last to move, to speak, to touch, she smoothed his black hair with her hand and let her eyes move over his face, trying to memorize each surface, each plane. "I think I know something else about you," she whispered huskily, then dropped tiny kisses along his neck and shoulders.

"What's that?" he asked lazily, sounding almost as if he really didn't care.

"Well, I hope it won't upset you, but I don't think you were a virgin."

His laughter filled the room, reached out and seemed to touch a clap of thunder, thus removing the fearsomeness from it. "Does that mean I did all right?" His tone was teasing.

"Oh, you definitely did all right." She kissed him lightly on the lips, then pulled his head to rest against her bosom once more.

"But you mustn't jump to hasty conclusions, Jackie. It could just be something that comes naturally to me."

"Undoubtedly," she murmured.

"Or it could have been beginner's luck."

"Could be. How on earth will we ever know?"

His hands and lips moved across all the concave and convex lines of her form, slowly rekindling sweet desire in her. Limbs tangled with limbs as she languidly, sensuously, moved with him, reveling in the mutually renewed arousal.

Suddenly Jackie gave a deep sigh and rolled away from Mark. The look she gave him was long and searching. "So much for all our noble resolves. I should have known when I brought you here. Perhaps, deep inside, I did. Not such a smart woman, am I?"

Mark smiled at her and smoothed her hair, testing each dark, silken strand against his fingers as if he drew some sort of comfort from the feel of it. "You're hair's so soft, so touchable. Like the rest of you."

"You're sidestepping my question," she pointed out, keeping well within his touch. She moved her hands across his chest and around to his back.

"When I woke up in that crummy hospital and saw

you standing there, I immediately wanted to make love to you. That was before I even had time to think about who or where I was. Even when the answers to those things did not come, I continued to want you with something akin to desperation. And whatever else I may turn out to be, I think I realize I'm not a humble sort. I've been able to see the attraction is mutual. The first few days . . . well, I worked at charming you. I couldn't believe this amnesia was going to last like this. Then when it did, I tried to back off. There were too many complications for involvement."

"And I wouldn't let you back off. Sorry?" She sat up slightly and looked down into his face. His hands reached up to cup her breasts and she bent her face toward his for a long, sweet kiss.

"At a time like this, how can I be sorry? Yet I'm scared for us, Jackie. I really am."

"Shhhh." She placed a finger against his lips. "Don't speak of it. Do you ever believe in fate, Mark? Nothing like this has ever happened to me before. Sure, in some ways, I've been 'involved' with my patients, but not like this. Not with such a maddening lack of logic. From the beginning, it was as if *we* were meant to be."

"I feel the same way. Just being around you evokes a tenderness in me that's almost frightening. I love you, Jacqueline. Whatever happens from here on out, remember that."

Being unable to bear all the talk of the future, of remembering, Jackie settled back down against Mark and kissed him deeply. Her kisses were moist and needful, her mouth felt burned and bruised from the hot, eager furnace that was his mouth. The playfulness subsided as the need mounted. Their movements became purely erotic. He claimed her again while the storm still raged.

When the lightning flashed, his face was lit with a look of love and desire that was the most wonderful sight she had ever seen. The sound of the rain against the roof and windowpane was a clear, free-swinging rhythm that their bodies kept pace with until the pleasure was so pure it could not be borne anymore—and they burst through to an ultimate surrender just as the heavens grew suddenly calm. The storm was over. The rain continued to fall steadily, peacefully.

"Don't leave me tonight, Mark," Jackie murmured.

"Of course not, darling. I'll be right here, just rest and sleep."

Safe and content, Jackie slept within the circle of his arm.

"Busy schedule today?" Mark asked from across the breakfast table.

"Pretty much so. But I'll take time out for lunch with you if you want to meet somewhere."

"No, that's okay. I'm doing some painting over at the Marshalls' house. I wouldn't look like much. An up-and-coming neurologist can't be seen in the company of a handyman."

"Don't be silly. It doesn't need to be anyplace fancy. We could even meet at the cafeteria in St. John's. There's something there I'd like you to see anyway."

"What time, then, my love?"

"One o'clock?"

"That's great. Actually, *I* have a busy schedule, too. While you're looking into brains, I'll be painting ceilings."

Jackie cast a swift and appraising look at Mark. She wondered if there was an edge of seriousness to his comment, if he were feeling "inferior" because of her position, but she elected to treat it as a jest. "Don't knock ceilings, Marcus. Take the Sistene Chapel, for instance. Just shows you what can be done."

"Uh-huh. I'm sure Michelangelo would appreciate the comparison with me. And I'm even surer the Marshalls would appreciate my artistic attempts on their ceilings."

As he talked, Jackie was thinking that he absolutely had to be the most devastatingly attractive man she had ever known. The thought caused her to wrinkle her nose flirtatiously at him.

"Are you toying with my affections, ma'am?" he asked, pulling his features into lines of mock sternness.

"I plead guilty."

"Good. Just promise you'll never stop."

They giggled together like a pair of kids until Jackie had to leave for morning rounds. This was definitely one Monday morning that wasn't a blue Monday, she thought. She had been in Mark's arms all night long and would be in them again tonight. That was enough to put a spring in any woman's step. While she worked, she wore a slightly smug, though pleasant smile on her face. She was very aware of her own body as she moved. It felt light, graceful, and marvelously sexy. One night of love with Male Patient Dolan and she could not imagine being without him. Caution, Jackie dear, she warned herself, although she knew it was much too late for caution. It had been too late for a long, long time. As they had discussed last night, there had been an inexplicable bond between them from the beginning. There had been a time when that bond could have been severed, but she had not even really tried to do so.

When Jackie saw Mark striding toward her across the cafeteria, her heart turned completely over. She could not believe the happiness she felt at the first sight of him. That same happiness was mirrored on his face. He wore the look of a man in love, and seeing that, she was flooded with a sense of peace and well-being.

"Tell me, doctor," he asked with boyish seriousness, "do you have much of a problem with patients falling head over heels in love with you?"

"Definitely," she teased. "It happens all the time. Especially the ones I take home with me."

"Hmmm, I see. Then do me a favor. Don't bring anyone else home. Under certain circumstances, I'm opposed to crowds. And sharing."

"Selfish brute."

"You better believe it. And how I wish we were somewhere else. I want to do things to you that wouldn't bear public scrutiny."

"Spare me the details. I don't believe I could stand the temptation. And I'd hate to create a scandal right here in St. John's cafeteria."

"St. John's a prude?"

"I wouldn't know. We've never met. But several of the employees are a bit stuffy."

Despite the "public scrutiny" of the crowded cafeteria, Mark reached out and lightly touched her face. He traced one finger along the slight tilt of her left eye. "Really, truly, my love, you're a pretty, pretty woman. Both exotic and vulnerable. Seriously, don't you have a problem with other male patients?"

Jackie laughed and squeezed his hand affectionately. "I've never been romantically involved with a patient before. Children like me. And old people. I've had young girls who seem to see me as an ideal of sorts, like a role model. Teenage boys and very young men get a bit shy and big-eyed in my presence. Goodness, Mark, all that makes me sound conceited. . . ."

"I find it fascinating. But what about the 'real' men?"

Jackie paused for a bite of lunch as she considered his question, then shook her head negatively. "Most 'real' men don't come to me as patients. They prefer 'real men doctors,' I guess. Truth is, I don't appeal to most men."

"I can't believe that. You'd turn heads in any crowd."

"Exactly. They turn toward, then away. Look up a list of the ten most desired traits in women—the dedication and ambition of a physician won't be among them."

"This conversation is beginning to sound familiar."

"You brought it up," she pointed out. "If you can think of something better to talk about, talk about it."

"How about our plans for tonight?" he asked with a suggestive leer.

"Let's stay on safe ground. Clean the tuna salad off your chin and I'll go show you our rehabilitation unit before we go back to work." In her love for him, she wanted him to know her other love—her work.

Mark walked down the halls with her to the elevator. As they ascended, Jackie was ever-conscious of his nearness and occasionally smiled up shyly into his face. She felt as young and vulnerable as a schoolgirl. They walked together easily, naturally. Before they entered the door of the rehabilitation department, he looked down into her face for a moment, his lips parted in a small smile, and suddenly Jackie remembered every glorious moment of the previous night, suddenly wanted him again.

"Anybody ever tell you that you're a sexy wench?" he whispered, his dark eyes sparkling with mischief and crinkling at the corners when he smiled.

"Well, certainly not under the present circumstances.

The corridors of St. John's aren't known as an atmosphere conducive to such observations."

His hearty laughter rang out. "I imagine you might be surprised, doctor, at some of the tales these corridors could tell."

"You could be right," she admitted with a laugh. "It's amazing what odd couples are often flushed out of the supply rooms at awkward moments. Anyway, enough of that. Come on in here."

Jackie showed Mark around the spacious room, where therapists worked in cubicles with patients. He seemed fascinated and genuinely interested in all she showed him.

"There's so much more we need," she told him, "in terms of equipment and audio-visual aids. Little money is allocated in the budget and we're dependent on donations. But a year or so ago we had nothing at all, so I'm pleased with the progress."

Mark watched the patients of all ages, shapes, and sizes. Some were struggling to walk, others to talk. Wasted limbs were being massaged. After they left the room, he asked questions about the scenes he had just witnessed. "What happened to the people, most of them?"

"Different things. The pretty woman is a stroke victim; she's still in her thirties and has children at home. It's been pretty tough for the whole family, but Linda's come a long way. She's having to learn how to talk and read all over again. The red-haired man had a tumor on his brain and the required surgery left him with some deficits. It will take a few more weeks of work, but he will eventually be able to return to his job. The young boy you saw . . . well, he's had no disease or accident as such, but his problem is a problem all the same. He's a stutterer."

"And the man who smiled all the time?"

"Hemiparesis. Another CVA—stroke, that is. That's not really a smile on his face; it's a distortion of the muscles and nerves. We're doing what we can for him, but understandably, he's depressed. Before he'll improve much, his attitude will have to change. Sometimes that doesn't happen."

Mark was very quiet as they walked to the car. When they reached it, Jackie turned to him. "See you tonight," she said gently, interrupting his reverie.

"Yeah. I was just thinking how lucky I am."

She did not have to ask what he meant. Losing one's past was not an easy situation to deal with but he had retained his full physical strength and the ability to learn and to reason.

When Jackie pulled into her garage that evening, she was slightly surprised to see the pickup truck was still gone. As usual, she was late getting home and she had expected Mark to be there. Most of his odd jobs did not keep him past five or six o'clock. She took a quick shower to rid herself of the medicinal smell that always seemed to cling to her after a day at the office and the hospital. After putting on a pair of white shorts and a red blouse, she went down to the kitchen to prepare the evening meal. She was looking through the refrigerator for needed items when Mark came in. He wore clean khakis and a white knit shirt, which was open at the throat; the color of the fabric was in striking contrast to the terrific tan he had acquired. He carried two boxes in his arms; one was square and flat and the other long and slender.

"Good," he said, positively beaming at her. "I caught

you before you really started anything. I've brought you gifts, my love."

"What sort of gifts? Though from the aroma, I can guess at one."

"Pizza for the stomach and roses for the soul."

He deposited both boxes on the kitchen table and Jackie lifted the lid of the florist's box to reveal the long-stemmed roses.

"American beauties," Mark informed her. "They reminded me of someone I knew. Can't think now who it was so I just brought them to you."

"With *your* memory, it's a wonder you remembered where to come."

"Come here and kiss me."

Without a protest, Jackie moved into his arms. It was like coming home.

"You feel so soft, so good," he murmured, then gave a laugh as his hands roamed down her back. "No wonder. Where's your bra?"

"I left it off. Weather's quite hot, you know." Quivers of delight ran up and down her spine as he lovingly nuzzled his face into the curve between her neck and shoulder.

"Only reason?" he teased, nibbling at her lips.

"How's 'easy access' for a reason?"

"Excellent. Top honors."

A few swift moves unfastened the buttons of her red blouse, and Mark pressed her tightly against him, flattening the fullness of her breasts against his chest.

"How do you feel about cold pizza?" he asked softly.

"It isn't one of my favorite things. Why do you ask?"

"Suddenly, for some peculiar reason, a need more urgent than hot food has arisen."

She felt his kiss again, firm and demanding, and an

answering urgency soared within her. She clung to him until they rocked and swayed with a mounting, primal need. Together they moved toward the stairs, pausing after each step to embrace and kiss again.

"Damn those stairs," he said huskily when they had reached their base. "It's such a long way up. Such a waste of time."

"Then don't bother," Jackie said, guiding him toward the living room, where they sank to the sofa and once again tasted the ecstasy of the previous night. When their passion was spent, they lay within each other's arms for a few minutes of gentle peace before they returned to the kitchen to attend to the neglected roses and pizza.

As soon as they were through eating, they went up to bed where they made love again, this time without haste. The rest of the night was spent in alternating bouts of peaceful sleep and sweet lovemaking.

Once Jackie got up and went to the bedroom window and looked out. A lone star twinkled in the dark Mississippi sky. "What are you doing over there?" Mark asked sleepily from the bed.

"Watching the star."

"Star? Just one star? At this time of night? You suppose it's still the first star of the evening?"

Jackie shrugged slightly. Her graceful form was silhouetted against the wall. Knowing the pleasure Mark found in her body, she walked in front of him unclothed with no sense of embarrassment. In the dim light, she appeared as esthetically pleasing and purely defined as a Grecian statue. "First. Last. Only. Anyway, it's all I see."

"Well, then, call it the first star and make a wish for me."

"What shall I wish for you?"

His answer came quickly. "That when my memory is restored, it will be a time of joy for both of us . . . that it will be something good."

"Do you worry about that?" she asked. *She* did, of course. The fear of losing Mark to his past was always with her, an ache surrounding the joy.

"Sure," he admitted. "After all, I might turn out to be someone you don't like."

"I don't think that will be the problem, Mark. You have a good heart, a fine soul. Those qualities won't alter when you assume a different name."

"That's another thing I wish for: that your faith in me will be justified. Now, come on back to bed. I miss you."

The next morning Jackie woke up before the alarm clock went off. Happiness flooded her with a singing purity when she saw that Mark had moved in his sleep until his dark head was nestled between her breasts. Being careful not to wake him, she reached over and shut off the alarm before it sounded. For the few moments left before she had to get up, she wanted simply to lie there with him asleep within her arms. Each time like this could easily be the last. Knowing that made it infinitely more precious.

Chapter Five

"You're sleeping with him, aren't you?" Marge asked. Her tone managed to be both matter-of-fact and accusing.

Jackie smiled to herself as she stirred the barbecue sauce. When she turned around, she managed to avoid looking directly at Marge. Instead she glanced out at the back patio where Rich and Mark were charcoal broiling the meat. The three small-sized McPhersons were providing lots of "help" and noise.

"Well, aren't you?" Marge insisted.

"Yes, Marge, I am. And enjoying it immensely." The radiant face she turned toward her friend was proof of her statement.

Marge regarded Mark through the window as he walked across the yard with two of the kids in tow. "I don't doubt that," she said with a sigh as her eyes swept across his wide-shouldered, lean-hipped frame. "And don't tell me it's none of my business. I know that already. But I'm uneasy, Jackie. I don't see how this can end well."

"As a matter of fact, neither do I."

Marge's carefully plucked eyebrows flew into arches of surprise. "You don't? I rather imagined you were telling yourself fairy tales."

"Oh, I tell them all right. But I've always known a fairy tale from the truth."

"Then why on earth let yourself in for . . ."

Jackie held up her hands in defense. "Please, Marge. For once in my life, I've thrown caution to the wind. And tomorrow I may, as the saying goes, 'inherit the wind.' But no more lectures. Let's just enjoy the evening, okay?"

Marge's face was full of skepticism, but being a good friend, she smiled and said, "Okay," and did not bring up the subject again. During the remainder of the evening, Jackie showed an open affection toward Mark. She was too much in love to attempt reticence. The growing despondency within made her treasure each moment.

"Have you ever remembered anything else, Mark?" Jackie asked. It had been a little over a week since his first memory and he had not mentioned the issue since. Jackie wondered if he knew how much courage it took for her to raise it. Maybe it was her imagination, but a veil seemed to cross his face, altering it somehow.

"Not much. Feelings more than actual memories. No names, nothing concrete. I remember a woman. . . ." He smiled tenderly at her expectant face. "I suppose she's my mother. Right now I seem to be stuck in early childhood. It will come, Jackie, it will come. And don't worry, love. I just don't believe I can be married, do you?"

"No, really, I can't. I suppose that's only wishful thinking. But you don't act like a husband. Not like any I've been around anyway. You know what I've been thinking, honey?"

"You want me to guess or what?"

"I could contact a parapsychologist for you."

"What do I need a 'pair of them' for? Am I that bad off?"

"You know what I mean. A clairvoyant."

"Do you believe that stuff?" he asked. He stretched out lazily and seemed to fill every inch of the red plush sofa in her study.

"Could be worth a try. The police and F.B.I use them often."

He shook his head rather vigorously. "That kind of stuff freaks me out. Let's just let nature take its course. Now, what are we going to read tonight?"

Jackie set down her bowl of popcorn and looked up at the bookshelves. "You pick." She felt almost relieved that he had refused to consult a parapsychologist, wanting what existed between them now to be without end.

"Gosh, how exciting. Ever notice how exciting our lives are?"

"I've noticed," she said with a smile. "We're becoming downright domesticated. If you'd like, we can do something different tonight, something exciting."

"Such as?"

"I could stay here alone and you could go out. . . ."

"So far this doesn't sound too great."

"Quit interrupting. You go to a telephone booth and call me. Then you can breathe heavily and say obscene things."

Mark laughed at her and held out his hand. "Come over here and sit by me."

With an exaggerated sigh, she said, "I guess this means you won't do it. Look how lazy you've become. Can't move a muscle to get off the couch."

But she went to him as he had known she would. He pulled her to him, then began panting audibly. When she giggled, he pulled her head down and whispered something delightfully naughty into her ear.

"See," he said, "it's better in person."

"If you say so. Now, what are we going to read?"

Their habit of reading aloud to each other had started even before they had become lovers. Using a wide variety of reading materials, the original intent was to inspire memories. Now it was something they enjoyed, something that had become a part of their life together.

Although he pretended it gave him great pain to do so, Mark did get up to look through the books. He selected a black-and-a-red bound volume of Edgar Allan Poe's works. A page at a time, they took turns reading two of the macabre stories to each other. "Had enough?" Mark asked when they had finished the second. "Poe wasn't exactly a pleasant man, was he?"

"No, not exactly. Only . . . look through the book, Mark. Before we quit, read me one more thing."

"And what do I get out of it?"

"The usual," she replied saucily.

"Hmmm. Good enough. What's the one more thing you want?"

" 'Annabel Lee.' I know it's in there. Find it and read it to me."

Mark hunted through the volume until he found the haunting, lyrical poem. " 'It was many and many a year ago, in a kingdom by the sea,' " he began. His voice was deep, resonant, and well modulated. He could be an actor, Jackie thought. He certainly has the looks, voice, and bearing for it. But soon she was caught up in the mood of the poem and it carried her along. He read the first four stanzas smoothly, not as if he were seeing the words for the first time. When he got down to the last two, Jackie was completely under the magic spell of the combined efforts of Mark and Poe.

> But our love it was stronger far than the love
>   Of those that were older than we—
>   Of many far wiser than we—
> And neither the angels in heaven above,
> Nor the demons down under the sea
> Can ever dissever my soul from the soul
>   Of the beautiful Annabel Lee:
>
> For the moon never beams, without bringing me dreams
>   Of the beautiful Annabel Lee;
> And the stars never rise, but I feel the bright eyes
>   Of the beautiful Annabel Lee;
>   And so, all the night tide, I lie down by the side
>   Of my darling—my darling—my life, and my bride,
>   In the sepulchre there by the sea—
>   In her tomb by the sounding sea.

By the time he reached the end, he was not reading anymore. He was looking deeply into Jackie's dark blue eyes and the words slipped from his lips effortlessly.

"You're not reading," she said.

"I know."

"Well, does it jog anything?"

"Jacqueline, love," he said tenderly, "every school kid's been exposed to Poe at one time or another. When I remember something significant, I'll let you know. In the meantime, don't worry? Okay?"

"Okay. That's a beautiful poem, isn't it?"

"Sure. But like the rest of his stuff, it's macabre, too."

"True. But that isn't what I like about it."

"And what is it you like?"

"Just the pure and lyrical quality of it. Plus, I suppose, proclamations of eternal, undying love appeal to my romantic side."

The smile he gave her was filled with such tenderness it caused her heart to give a little leap. " 'And neither the angels in heaven above, nor the demons down under the sea, can ever dissever my soul from the soul of the beautiful Jacqueline Marie.' "

"There. I like that."

"And it's true, you know. I can't imagine anyone ever being able to dissever my soul from yours."

"Just let 'em try," she said dramatically and defiantly, but further foolish words were stopped when his lips sealed hers. The long night stretched ahead of them. There was lots of time for making love without hurry. Mark scooped her up in his arms and carried her up the long staircase.

"Look at me," she told him with a pleased smile. "Scarlett O'Hara has nothing on me."

Mark deposited her on the bed somewhat ungraciously, then sank beside her with an exaggerated groan. "Wonder if Rhett Butler's back hurt this bad? Maybe you should check into Scarlett's diet."

"Complaining?"

His hands began to move skillfully over the now familiar contours of her body. "Ask that question again an hour or so from now."

Much later that night, after desire had ebbed and flowed and finally subsided into a gentle peace, Jackie awoke and immediately noticed Mark was not in bed with her. She got up and went downstairs. When she saw him in the study, she started to go in, then stopped. From where she stood, she could see him but he could not see her. He had turned on a small reading lamp and its artificial light glared harshly. Although he held a book in his hand, he was not reading. His strong, regular features could have been carved from stone at that moment, so stern were they. His face was a distant and very contemplative mask. Jackie was positive that he was remembering something. It occurred to her that he may have been recalling more lately, gradually, than he had let her know.

An indescribable sadness seized her heart. Knowing she should not intrude on his privacy, she turned and went back up the stairs. The large bed in which she had been sleeping since she bought the old house nearly two years ago seemed terribly lonely. It was a very long time before Mark came back to bed. He moved quietly, slipping in beside her with stealthy consideration. Although she did not let him know she was awake, she rolled over against him and felt contentment once more when he placed his arm around her. She liked the way he did that, tightly enough to seem loved, loosely enough to preclude possessiveness. The words of Poe's haunting poem echoed through her mind, and repeating them over and over to herself, she was finally able to sleep.

"I don't think I want to go, Jacqueline."

"Oh, come on, Mark," she pleaded. "That's what you said about the dinner at the McPhersons', and now you get along with them quite well."

His answer was short. "This is different."

"Nonsense. I don't go in for parties and gala festivities myself, but this is almost compulsory. It's a big fund-raising affair for the hospital. And as you've seen for yourself, St. John's certainly needs funds."

"Old-time Mississippi riverboat festival? Sounds a bit corny."

"But that isn't why you object to going, is it?"

Mark smiled at her, but Jackie was well acquainted now with the variety of his expressions, and *this* smile was somewhat strained.

"I don't have the right kind of clothes."

"It's a costume-ball-type thing. The right kind of suit can be bought or rented."

"With your money, undoubtedly."

"Oh, Mark, get off this kick. Even at the kind of work you're doing now, you make enough to rent a costume. And even if I *did* have to pay for it, so what? We both know this situation is temporary, that when your memory comes back . . ."

"Don't you mean 'if,' not 'when'?"

"I meant exactly what I said. Now, if you don't want to go, fine. I'll get another date. But I *have* to go and I won't go alone. Suit yourself. I won't ask you again." Rather huffily, she turned back to the hated job of scrapping old paint off the wall. She moved the scraper down with a vicious movement.

"Hey, watch it, you'll cut yourself. Take it slow and easy with that thing."

"You an expert?" she asked sarcastically.

"As a matter of fact, I am. I'm becoming quite good at this odd-job bit."

"Jolly."

"By the way, Jackie, I have an idea for your kitchen. . . ."

Jackie turned away from her task to look at him for a moment. Even in faded navy-blue tennis shorts and a white T-shirt, he was a marvel to behold. She felt herself melting into mush. What did it really matter if he consented to go to a dumb party or not? The important thing was that he was here with her, loving her. Having him around—how vital that had become to her well-being.

"I can't afford ideas for my kitchen," she said, knowing the husky timbre of her voice revealed her return to tenderness toward him.

"This one's free," he said proudly. "Where I'm working now, over at the Dayton farm, there's an old brick shed way out in the back. They'd like to use the area for something else, so if I'll tear it down and haul the bricks away; I can have them. They're really old—pre-Civil War. It's a great find, Jackie. I've been reading up on it, looking in books of all sorts, and I know the perfect way to do the walls of your kitchen."

"But, Mark, that would be so much work for you."

"I want to do something to repay all your kindness, Jackie. This is only a little thing, a beginning. But I know I can do it. . . . Here, I'll be right back."

She heard him running up the stairs swiftly, taking them two at a time. When he returned, he took a can of beer from the refrigerator and offered her one. She had never learned to like the stuff and shook her head in refusal, choosing a soft drink instead.

With the look of a small boy offering a pretty wild flower, he handed her some drawings.

"These are marvelous, Mark," she said as she scanned them.

"I know," he agreed immodestly.

His drawings were very detailed, and she could tell quite clearly what he meant to do. She could picture the old, faded bricks covering most of the walled surfaces, a few places left painted or wallpapered for contrast. A unique brick archway was shown over the range with the lighting and fan recessed up inside it.

"Where do these neat wooden cabinets come from?" she asked wryly.

"Well, you see . . ." he began, his face radiant with a genuine ear-to-ear grin.

"Don't tell me: you know where you can get this free wood and you read this book on cabinet making."

"Close enough. You're a smart woman. Ever consider being a doctor?"

Suddenly tired, she stretched her aching back and leaned up against the old, battered kitchen cabinet.

"What do you think? You mind if I give it a try?" Mark asked eagerly. Jackie realized the project meant a lot to him. He had put so much work and thought into the project before even mentioning it to her. He had wanted to surprise her, to offer this as a gift.

"It would please me very much. This room has so much potential, I shudder when I look at its present state. So if you want to do it and it isn't too much work, then have at it."

"Great." Carrying his beer can with him, he moved toward her and took her in his arms. "How about a kiss to seal the bargain?"

"Yuck," she said when his face came toward hers, "I can't stand the smell of beer. I suppose that's why I don't drink it."

He laughed and took another big drink, after which a speck of foam clung to his upper lip. "No kisses for me tonight? Not even one?" he teased, his arms cradling her, his very nearness evoking warm sensuality in her. Tentatively, she kissed his upper lip, licking the trace of foam off with her tongue. Then she explored his mouth more fully, the pungent taste and smell of the beer assailing her senses. Within a few moments, she was reeling with a heady, dizzying sensation. This feeling was due entirely to his overwhelming masculinity, which was more intoxicating than any liquor ever brewed.

No more paint was to be scraped that night.

Much later, she stretched lazily across the bed, her limbs still warm and tingly from their recent entwinement with Mark's.

"You really going to find another date for that party?" he asked, his lips finding a favorite spot on her throat.

"Probably. Maybe 'date' is the wrong word. An escort is what I need. Strictly platonic."

"I should hope so. Though I can't see why any man in his right mind would consent to a platonic relationship with you. Nonplatonic is much nicer."

"Ain't it though," she drawled, curling against him, ready to sleep.

When her lids were heavy and her whole being was relaxed, he said softly, "I'll go. I'll be your escort."

"You don't need to do that, Mark. Not if you'd hate it."

"It's okay. I was just being stubborn, I guess. Only I want it understood I'm no platonic escort."

"It's understood. I love you. Good night."

"In other words, 'shut up and go to sleep'?" he asked with a laugh.

"You got it," she replied sleepily, then gave a sigh of contentment as peace and darkness met and merged. It was one of the rare moments when she was able to let go of her fears, to truly live for the present.

"You're beautiful," Mark said simply.

"And so are you."

Dressed in their costumes for the riverboat party, they made a striking couple. Mark wore a white suit and ruffled shirt. Once he had decided to go through

with the party, he had fitted himself out to the hilt.
From the toe of his shining boots to the tip of his rakish,
wide-brimmed white hat, he was a Mississippi gambler.
A very real-looking dark mustache had "grown" on his
upper lip. A multitude of gaudy, jeweled rings were on
his fingers.

Thinking that most of the ladies would wear white,
ruffled gowns, Jackie had chosen one of garnet red. The
richly colored material was filmy and draped beautifully
over the full crinoline she wore beneath it. The bodice
fit tightly to emphasize her slender waistline and was
quite low cut; only by arranging the filmy ruffles discreetly did she manage to cover most of her bosom so
that only enough showed to tantalize the viewer.

She had curled her hair more than usual, pulling it
back into an old-fashioned style. She had experimented
with putting it up on top of her head but Mark hadn't
liked that. He preferred gentle curls cascading to her
shoulders, shot through with strands of red ribbon. The
soft femininity of the hairstyle gave the right touch to the
dress. Tonight she was Scarlett O'Hara before the war
and poverty had touched her: bright, flirtatious, and
lovely; the cream of southern society.

On the way out the door, Mark disarranged her ruffles long enough to place warm kisses in the cleft formed
by her breasts. "We could just stay home," he murmured.

"No way," she said with a laugh, modestly covering
her chest as much as the dress would allow. "I want all
the women there to see my own private riverboat gambler and eat their hearts out."

"Well, in that case, the least I can do is make an
appearance." He gave a courtly bow, then took her
hand and escorted her out to the car.

When they approached the pier where a huge white

riverboat, *Mississippi Lady*, rode the dark water, Mark looked up at it with a rather strange expression on his face. Many of the guests had already arrived and the merry chatter of voices and laughter was randomly interwoven with the music from the band. The lights from the high, narrow windows of the riverboat threw out beams of yellow. Mark muttered something Jackie did not quite catch; it sounded like, "This looks familiar," but when she asked him to repeat it, he ignored her request. Instead he took her arm and guided her up onto the *Mississippi Lady*.

"Dr. Jacqueline Spencer and Mr. Mark Dolan," announced the blue-coated usher when they entered the elaborately decorated room. A few sharp intakes of breath were audible as they glided across the floor, and Jackie's cheeks glowed with a high natural color elicited by the spontaneous compliment. She had been correct in guessing that white dresses would dominate the scene. Among all the billowing gowns of virginal paleness, her red frock glowed like a solitary ruby in a field of pearls. A quick look around the ballroom enhanced her pleasure, for her escort was the most handsome man present.

"You dance well," she commented as they moved to the music.

"It's easy when your partner is the prettiest woman in the room."

For the next hour or so, they danced, chatted with other people, sipped a little champagne, and nibbled at the canapés. Several times Jackie danced with other men she knew. Mark gallantly asked their female companions to dance, though Jackie noted he kept looking over at her. He did not appear to be jealous of her partners, merely somehow lost and forsaken because she was not with him. The idea of this filled her with a rush of tenderness. She shouldn't, she thought, have asked him to come. He knew none of these people well, and considering his amnesia, he hadn't much of a supply of small talk to offer. But he knew a few of them, she mused, and the thought was an uncomfortable one. The woman Mark was talking to at the moment, Jackie saw, was Paula Hodges. Mark had washed her cars, cleaned out her garage, and resurfaced her patio.

"Having fun?" he asked Jackie when she was happily restored to his arms and was being whirled across the dance floor to the beat of a fast and happy song.

She looked about the crowded room. The people seemed somehow exaggerated. They were drinking too much, talking too rapidly, laughing too loudly. It was as if they were forcing themselves to have a good time.

"It's been fun, in a way," she told Mark at last. "To get all dressed up and enter into the spirit of the thing, slip back to a bygone era. But it's not my cup of tea—not really. I'd rather be home with you, papering a bedroom or reading out loud. In fact, I think I'd even rather be seeing patients. Dreadfully dull of me, I suppose."

Mark did not say anything else, just skillfully moved across the floor, dipping and swaying with easy masculine grace. After the dance ended, she excused herself to go to the ladies' room. When she returned a few minutes later, she did not see Mark anywhere.

"Care to dance," Dr. Vonkleman asked. "They're playing a slow one and that's the only kind I can do."

And even those are painful for your partner's feet, Jackie thought. But she smiled charmingly and accepted her colleague's offer. Harv lived up to her expectations, and she practically limped away when the music ended. She saw Mark striding toward her across the shining floor and she began to smile, as she always did when she caught sight of him. But the smile faded quickly when she saw that his usually genial features were distorted into a terrible mask of anguish.

"What's wrong?" she asked in alarm.

"Jackie, I have to get the hell out of this place. Right now. If you want to stay, I'll catch a taxi. You're under no obligation to leave. But I have to get out before I kill somebody."

He turned on his heels and strode out angrily. For a moment, Jackie was too stunned to act. She stood staring after him until he disappeared through the doorway, then ran toward the door herself. Despite her surprise and confusion, she was aware of the nervous tittering in the room that followed her out the door. Something was definitely going on that she didn't know about.

"Mark," she called, "wait up. I'll go with you." His white-suited figure was halfway down the pier but he did pause and wait. When she drew nearer, the grimness of his face was apparent. "Are you going to tell me what's the matter?"

"Can't you guess, Jacqueline? Are you really that naive?"

She moved her shoulders in a gesture of exasperation. The carefully arranged silken ruffles fell away and the swell of her breasts was clearly visible in the combined light of the moon and the boat dock. He glanced down at her face and pretty bosom with a look that approached derision.

"I guess I can be, Mark," she said quietly, "because I certainly have no idea what happened back there."

He drew a deep breath and continued to stare at her. It was as if he were seeing her for the very first time.

She had the impression he didn't like what he saw and fear rose within her, making her almost nauseous.

When she dared to speak, she knew her voice was shaky. "Let's walk, Mark. The evening has grown nice and cool. It's lovely out here by the sound. Come on, let's walk and talk about it."

They walked along in uneasy silence. When they reached a place where onlookers could lean against a railing over the water, she stopped. "Mark," she began, her impatience showing in the way she spoke his name.

"You really don't know, do you?" he asked.

"That's what I keep telling you."

He gripped the metal railing so hard his knuckles went white. "You're an educated and wealthy professional woman, Jackie. . . ." he began.

"I'm not wealthy, not really," she protested.

He cut her off rudely. "We're speaking relatively. Relative to me, that is. I'm an anonymous bum, a doer of odd jobs, an recipient of charity really. That makes us a rather odd pair."

"But, Mark . . ."

" 'But, Mark' nothing. There's a name—an ugly name—for men who live off wealthy, lonely women."

"You're not living off me."

"Aren't I? How well could I make it alone on what I get paid for mowing lawns and weeding gardens? The word, my dear, is 'gigolo.' And I heard it used tonight. About me. More than once, and clearly spoken so that I couldn't miss it."

Jackie's nausea increased. The lights and shadows cast upon the waters of the Mississippi Sound were beautiful and romantic, and these qualities were only enhanced by the distant sounds of the band. But this ambience didn't touch her; none of it mattered. Mark's words slapped her forcefully, leaving her feeling bruised, hurt, and withdrawn. She could think of nothing to say.

"Damn it all anyway. It's close to the truth," Mark said and struck a clenched fist against the metal railing with a force that made it shake and vibrate.

"Let's go home," she said dully. She walked toward the car and got in on the driver's side. When he wordlessly got in on the other side, she was not surprised. Neither would she have been surprised if he had refused to come with her. She had to mash the dress and crinoline down mercilessly before she could drive, but that didn't matter. The party was most definitely over.

When Mark spoke, he sounded cryptic. "I could have driven."

"You're too upset. And it doesn't matter about the dress, not now."

"Suit yourself.

Nothing else was said during the drive. Once they were safe inside the part-shabby, part-beautiful mansion that had become their home, she confronted him. "Aren't you overreacting to this just a bit?"

"Didn't you have some idea what kind of talk you were setting yourself up for with this situation, Jacqueline?"

"Hey, that's no fair, answering a question with a question." Her attempt at light banter fell flat and left an empty sound in the air.

"Oh, hell, there's no use talking about this. I didn't want to come back here tonight. But I didn't know what else to do. There's a limit to what a man can get by with in an outfit like this. Even in Biloxi, Mississippi." With vicious movements, he threw the hat across the room, then jerked the mustache off his lip.

"Please, Mark," she pleaded, "calm down and talk sensibly." When she touched his arm, she felt quite timid. This overwrought man was not the easygoing one she knew and loved. He withdrew from her light touch coldly.

"Go on to bed, Jackie. Maybe we'll talk later. But I'm not sleeping with you tonight, so don't wait up."

"Are you leaving?" Fear lay heavily across her chest.

"Not tonight." A certain weariness had returned to his voice.

"Mark, I need you with me."

His dark eyes roamed insolently down her lovely red-clad figure. "Sorry, doctor, the stud service is closed. Even we gigolos need a night off now and then."

Jackie reached out to slap him, but he caught hold of her wrist and stopped her. For a long moment, he stared into her eyes, which had turned a darker blue with pain, and then he dropped her wrist.

Suddenly she was angry, not hurt. She spoke with carefully measured words. "You refer to yourself as a gigolo. What does that make me? Do you see me as a woman so desperate for a lover that she has to buy one under the pretext of offering him shelter and help when he's in trouble?"

"The situation does seem to fit uncomfortably well, doesn't it?" he replied. "There's nothing like casual onlookers' observations to make one take a good, long look at oneself."

"Your portrait of me is quite flattering." She uttered a short, mirthless laugh.

"What did you expect, Jackie? What would you say of another woman who opened her home to someone like me? Would you automatically assume all the intentions were pure?"

"They were," she insisted stubbornly.

"My dear, we wanted each other badly from first sight. Do you deny that?"

It took a great deal of strength to look him in the eye, but she managed the feat. "I do not deny the attraction, yet I never regarded it as a cheap attraction. My main concern was to help you. Maybe love stirred in me from the beginning as well as desire. Whatever the reason, I couldn't bear to see you turned over to social services. I talked myself into believing I was strong enough to resist my 'baser urges.' As we can see, I was wrong."

"Very wrong." His features were stony. Everything about him was dark and unreadable. "You're an intelligent woman, but you fell headlong into a not-so-smart situation. We should have known from the beginning we were headed for disaster. God, there's no way out. Because we didn't know what the return of my memory would bring, I've almost hoped at times I'd never remember anything. But then I'd always be a kept man, wouldn't I? It would have been better if I had just gone to social services. Then, I would have saved us from all this."

"I'm sorry. I truly am." It took all of the dignity Jackie possessed to turn and walk slowly across the room, then up the stairs without a backward glance.

Her bed was an island of loneliness. She did not want lovemaking. Indeed, she had never felt less sexy in her life, but she had a real need for Mark to hold her and love her. Trying to think objectively, she could understand his reaction. Everything he had undergone so recently had been emotionally taxing on the man. Nevertheless, her hurt was so deep she really couldn't be objective.

She did not sleep, nor did she cry. Although crying

might have provided some release, tears did not come. When morning arrived at last, the shadows beneath her eyes were like bruises. The truck and car were both in the garage but Jackie did not try to locate Mark. Remembering that she had a critically ill patient to check at the hospital, she dressed casually and left the house. The patient's condition had stabilized and she was not at St. John's long. She bought a cup of coffee from a vending machine and carried it with her to the car, wanting to escape the hospital before she ran into someone she knew and had to make conversation. Driving around the streets of Biloxi, she felt desolate. The hot coffee warmed her body but not her soul.

Parking on a side street, she rested her forehead against the steering wheel. "Oh, God, please. I love him so." The words echoed in her brain like a litany. Finally, the healing tears came. She let them flow for a long, long time. When she was composed, she turned on the ignition and started home.

Looking wan and forlorn in jeans and a pink shirt, she still had an innate dignity when she entered the kitchen. If she was surprised to see Mark there laying bricks, she did not show it.

"That's looking very nice," she commented. Although she imagined her face still showed traces of her recent tears, she did not try to hide it from him. Instead she looked at him directly, with pride and defiance. He was the one to waiver. She nodded slightly and left the room.

Kicking off her shoes when she reached her bedroom, she fell across her bed fully clothed. She wanted to lose herself in sleep. How long she slept she did not know. When she woke up, Mark was looking at her from the doorway.

"That's all I can do for the day. I ran out of mortar."

"Quite all right. Even God rested on Sunday." Not being able to bear looking at him, she rolled over and closed her eyes. Soon she heard water running in another part of the house. A few moments later Mark was back, wearing nothing but a towel knotted at his waist. He sat down on the bed and gripped her shoulders firmly but tenderly.

"Forgive me, darling. It's been a rough time for me—for both of us. But I went completely off my rocker last night. There's no excuse for the things I said to you. What I did was unforgivable, I know. But, please, I am sorry."

That was all it took; one "forgive me" and all the anger evaporated. She reached up and pulled him down to her, her fingers locking in the strands of his shower-dampened hair. In the glory of his kiss, she found the warmth, comfort, and love she needed so badly. He responded with increasing demand until her lips felt bruised and swollen.

When she finally pulled away and started to remove her clothing, he held her hands. "Let me do that, let me do it all." His voice was low, sweet, husky, and incredibly exciting. With slow deliberation, he made love to her exquisitely. She caressed his back and chest tenderly at first but as the crescendo of passion increased, her nails dug deeply into his flesh. She had thought they had experienced all there was to experience in sensuality. Now she knew she was wrong, for when he claimed her, it was with infinite depths of mastery and love. Having tasted bitterness and near-loss, realizing the precariousness of the future, they entered a new dimension. Insatiable, he led her through an endless maze of peaks and valleys. The words they spoke were pulled from near-delirium and the poignancy of their shared desperation fueled the mounting need.

"Oh, Mark, oh, love, like that," she cried, and was able to speak no more. A sound like the surf pounded in her ears and it was as if she were engulfed by the ocean itself—wild, tumultuous, and unbearably sweet. She held him tightly against her until the ocean had receded and she was on solid earth once more.

"Forgive me?" he murmured again next to her ear, nibbling at the tiny pearl earring she wore there.

"You have a pretty good argument going for you," she said with a laugh, then spoke with more seriousness. "We do have to talk about this, Mark. I've been like an ostrich as far as your amnesia is concerned. To be completely honest, I've feared the full return of your memory. But you have to try, you have to push for it. And if I can help, I will. We have to get this settled. I hope there's a future for us together. If not, we'll have to bear it. But we do have to find out."

"Thank you," he murmured, his lips moving softly against her palm.

"For what?"

"Mostly just for being you. And, Jackie, I want to be totally honest with you. I've been remembering little things. Maybe that's part of the reason I went so haywire last night. It's been nearly two months since the accident. That terrible three-month limit you mentioned is closing in. And we know things can't go on like this. I want you as a permanent part of my life, for us to build a forever. I'm sorry for last night. I know there's no buying and selling between us. Still, I have pride enough to know I can't marry you, not the way things are. A half-witted handyman and a neurologist. Some pair."

"Don't say things like that."

"Yet, love, there's a certain truth . . ."

"But not 'half-witted.' That's a terrible word."

"Okay," he said with a laugh. "Anyway, what I started to say is that all of that turmoil last night—that party and my reaction to it—it's started things working faster than they ever have. But I'm not ready to talk about it yet. I want to get it straighter in my mind, find out a few things on my own before I tell you anything else. Can you accept that?"

"I can accept anything except your not loving me. I'm prepared to lose you if I have to, as long as I know you still love me."

"Our souls will never be dissevered," he reminded her gently.

"Good enough. Now, seems to me my nap got interrupted. Care to join me?"

"Couldn't run me off if you tried."

Curved together spoon fashion, they slept the lazy Sunday afternoon away.

Chapter Six

❦

During the next few days, Mark was very loving and kind, although unusually quiet. The emotional turmoil that had occurred the night of the charity ball had been unsettling for them both. Having much to contemplate herself, Jackie did not question his mood. She did not even question it when he stopped taking odd jobs and devoted all of his time to the remodeling of her kitchen. She was amazed at the skill he exhibited in this endeavor, for she would have wagered he was not a man accustomed to manual labor. Anything he wanted to do, he could do, she thought, and was immediately possessed of an inner glow of pride.

Although the days were still quite hot, there was a definite hint of autumn in the early-morning and late-evening air. One cool morning, as she was leaving for work, Mark asked, "Do you think you'll be late tonight?"

She was somewhat surprised at the question, as he had long ago accepted her inability to arrive home at a certain time. Seeing the quizzical look that passed over her face, he smiled. "No special reason. I'd like to take you someplace nice for dinner if you're not too late or too tired. But if you are, don't worry. We'll make it another time."

"Sounds nice. I'll try."

They embraced briefly and Jackie walked toward the door. For some reason, unknown even to her, she paused and looked back at him for a moment. Standing there in his mortar-splattered shirt and jeans, his hair not really combed, he looked infinitely dear. How much longer? she wondered. How much longer until their idyllic interlude would alter, perhaps evaporate altogether.

Just as it was beginning to look as if she might get through with her patients at a reasonable hour, the telephone rang. Before she gave her name and reason for calling, Jackie recognized the voice of Dr. Beverly Cantrell, a pediatrician who was also on the staff at St. John's.

"Jackie? I hate to ask and I know I still owe you a favor from that stint you did for me in June, but . . ."

"But what, Bev?" she asked, unable to keep the weariness from her voice.

"I'm here at the free clinic and you wouldn't believe the number of kids they have lined up for me to see. And I am so sick I can barely stand up. Truly I am. In fact, if you can come out, I want you to check *me* first and write me a script so I can go home to get well or die in peace. Whichever comes first."

Knowing some of the tricks her colleagues had pulled to get out of unpleasant duties in the past, Jackie was dubious. She also knew she would do it anyway.

After she had arrived at the clinic and talked with Beverly, she was somewhat ashamed of her suspicion. Beverly had a fever of 103, and from even a cursory examination, it was clear she was not faking. Jackie gave her an injection and wrote out a prescription for her to have filled on the way home, then turned her attention to the bevy of small children lined up for "Well Baby Day."

This procedure consisted of checking for any defects or illnesses and to see that immunizations were current. Usually she enjoyed the work and the examinations were quickly done. Today, however, was a bit more difficult. First, she was faced with an unusually heavy load of cases. Second, several of the children had problems requiring referrals to various specialists.

When six o'clock had come and gone and she still had numerous children to check, she took a break to drink a cup of coffee and call Mark. She apologized to him and explained what had happened. He was calm and understanding, although disappointed. On impulse, she said, "Why don't you come down here and wait for me? After I'm done, we can still go somewhere to eat, even if it isn't someplace fancy."

He agreed and said he would be there a little later. Busy with her examinations, she was almost taken by surprise when she walked down the hall of the clinic and looked up to see him waiting in the lobby. She looked down at herself ruefully. The white smock, which had been crisply white at the beginning of the day, was now wrinkled and somewhat grayish. A medicinal smell seemed to cling to her hair and clothing, and she regretted being unable to shower and change before going out with Mark.

When he caught sight of her, he flashed his familiar brilliant smile. One small child left the examining area and another entered it. Several children of various ages, sizes, and colors were still in the waiting area. Catching on to the fact that Jackie was seeing them, he raised his eyebrows in a silent query. She wrinkled her nose and blew a kiss to him, uncaring that the little patients and their parents saw her.

An hour or so later, she was ready to go. It was eight-fifteen. She took off the dingy white coat and threw it across her arm. Even if she smelled antiseptic, she felt she at least looked fresher in the pale yellow shirt and tan skirt the smock had covered.

"Already?" Mark asked mockingly, throwing down a six-month-old magazine.

"They don't call me 'Speedy' for nothing."

"Actually, I've never heard anyone call you 'Speedy' at all."

As Jackie opened the car door to throw her soiled smock into the back, she heard someone call, "Hi, Miss Doctor." She turned to see a small, round face beaming at her; the little boy's brown eyes positively sparkled with pleasure at seeing "his doctor" outside the office. She talked to him briefly, causing him to duck his head rather shyly. After he and his mother were gone, Jackie slid into the car beside Mark.

"I had no idea there were that many kids with neurological problems," he said. "Why, some of them were just infants."

Jackie looked at him and gave a small laugh. "I guess I didn't explain well on the phone. I was substituting for Bev Cantrell and she's not a neurologist. She's a pediatrician. Most of the kids I saw this evening are prefectly normal, healthy little brats. We're just trying to keep them that way."

He shook his head in seeming dismay. "You're a pushover, Jacqueline."

"She was sick." Mark shot her a look brimming with skepticism. "She really was. I checked her myself. That's the way it is with my life, Mark, I can't help it. Or maybe I don't want to help it. You've never said anything before. Do you find yourself minding it now?"

He reached out and patted her affectionately. "Not for my sake, darling. But I worry about you sometimes. Up at six o'clock, still working after eight. And what and when was lunch?"

"I'm tough, I can take it. But I will admit I am ravenous. Let's go find someplace quick."

If Mark had wanted to go somewhere elegant to dine, Jackie knew he must feel let down. They found an informal steak house where the food was excellent, the service was good, and the atmosphere was relaxed. The quietness Jackie had noted in Mark recently persisted throughout the meal. Now, however, she was beginning to grow slightly apprehensive. There had always been times between them when they were silent and introspective, but the mood had been comfortable. This evening uneasiness hovered like a fog.

Once she touched his hand in mute appeal. His responsive smile was lavish in warmth. Whatever was wrong, he still loved her. She was certain of that.

"Want a drink?" Mark asked when they got home. "Soothe your nerves and settle your dinner."

"Bad habit."

"Once isn't a habit."

"Okay, fix me a brandy. I'm going to run up and slip into something more comfortable."

While she was changing into her pink nightgown and robe, her heart was beating rapidly. Cardiac palpitations, she thought wryly. Her imagination was running rampant. Mark had been so brooding and quiet and now he was practically insisting she have a drink. Add those factors to the general atmosphere and she knew he was getting ready to tell her something. She removed the barrettes and pins that held her hair away from her face during the day and slowly brushed it until it was a silken mantle, resting softly against her shoulders, its color as rich and pure as polished mahogany.

She found him in her study, the room where they had laughed, read, studied, talked, and loved. His smile, when he handed her the glass of amber liquid, was almost too kind, too considerate. The glass he retained himself was nearly empty. She wondered if that were his first drink, then somehow doubted it.

"Mark," she said, setting her glass down untouched, "you might as well tell me what you have to say now and get it over with."

"What makes you think . . .?"

Jackie's unique blue eyes looked gravely into his much darker ones. He grinned sheepishly and let his gaze drop away. "I guess I did promise you I'd be honest in this situation."

"And anesthetizing me with liquor probably won't help. Come on now, out with it. You've remembered everything, including a wife and numerous children, plus countless debts in Peoria?"

"Peoria?" he asked, looking tragic and comic at the same time.

"In Illinois. On a farm."

The smile he gave her was crooked and halfhearted. He refilled his glass and quickly drained it again. "No, Jacqueline, I'm not a Peorian farmer. I'm a Bostonian Giles Hafferty."

Her fingers grabbed the arm of the red sofa in a fierce grip. She seemed to feel herself grow pale, all blood draining from her face. And so he was no longer her Mark. One phase of their life was over—perhaps all phases. She did not speak, but her pretty, finely drawn features were beseeching.

"I'm not married. That's the first thing I asked."

"Asked? Whom did you ask?" Jackie was growing more bewildered. Mark—or whoever he said he was—did not seem too elated.

"The name came to me several days ago. Not long after all that row we had. I wanted to be sure of a few things before I told you. Even after I knew my name, I brooded for some time before I took action. I kept hoping it would all come back since I had that big clue. And it is gradually coming back. What I did yesterday, however, was go to the police and have them 'find' me. You've never heard that name?"

Feeling somewhat numb, Jackie shook her head slowly. "But I don't think I know *anyone* from Boston. And the name Hafferty isn't familiar at all. Why, are you famous?"

"The police seemed impressed." He was trying to smile, but the results were poor.

"What happens from here?"

"Jackie, this is all so weird. I've grown so used to being Mark Dolan. Now I'm going to have to get used to something else. Only I was *comfortable* being Mark. Even with all the obvious problems it created. It's a bit terrifying. What if I'm not comfortable being myself, being this Giles person. I mean, what kind of name is that? You know anyone else named that?"

Jackie had had about all of this she could bear. She laughed at him softly and held out her arms. "Whoever you are, come sit with me. You don't have to stand way over there all by yourself."

He did walk toward her, but filled his glass again before doing so. After he had sipped at it a bit, she insisted he take off his shoes and stretch out on the sofa with his head in her lap.

"Take your time telling me about it. Actually I think Giles is a rather nice name. Very British, very classy and aristocratic." All the while she talked, her fingers touched his hair, his forehead, and the soft, warm hollows behind his ears.

"This gets even weirder," he warned.

"That's okay," she soothed. "In neurology, one gets accustomed to weirdness."

"Well, I talked to my mother today."

"I suppose she's been worried sick."

She felt the movement of his shoulders against her thighs as he shifted position slightly. "Not really. Now that she knows of the amnesia and injury, she's concerned. But ol' Giles had a way of disappearing now and then anyway. Thus no hue and cry when this happened. Not much was said. Someone from the corporation is coming after me. I don't really feel too keen on going, but it's something I have to do."

"Corporation?"

"That's what the lady said. Remember, one of the first things I recalled was that I thought I had been rich. Well, I guess I am. And 'rich' may be an understatement. There's still a lot about it I don't know. Hopefully, my return to Boston, 'Mother,' and the old environment will 'retrieve my memories,' as you once said, more quickly than they've been retrieved so far."

"That's nice for you to be rich," she said rather woodenly.

"Yes, isn't it, though? Jackie, you don't remember hearing the name Giles Hafferty? Have you heard of Hafton Steel? Au Claire Cosmetics? Marchand Oil? Bigelowe Enterprises? Gemini Recordings? I could name more. In fact, I wrote them down somewhere. At 'Mother's' suggestion."

Jackie's hands flew to her mouth and she chewed at a thumbnail nervously, an old habit she had broken except during times of extreme stress.

"Oh, God, Mark. You own all that?"

His expression was grim. "Heir apparent to the largest blocks of stock in them all."

"Then why don't you sound happy? At least this gets you off the 'gigolo' hook."

Mark had to laugh at that and he moved his head so that he was looking up at her. "My pretty, pretty doctor with the zany, wonderful sense of humor that serves her on any occasion. Okay, so being rich shouldn't be a problem. I guess, to put it bluntly, I'm not looking forward to this venture. It isn't something I can explain."

"I think I know. We've shared so much, built a warm little cocoon about us. And now that's over and done with. No matter how nice it was at times, it was only temporary shelter."

"Nicely put. . . . I guess the timing is as good as possible. They're arriving for me tomorrow afternoon. I think I can put the finishing touches on your kitchen in the morning. Come to Boston with me, Jackie?"

He asked the question lightly, but she knew it carried some importance. She gave the answer she had to give, the one he was expecting. "I don't think so. I'm heavily scheduled and it would be difficult to get away. If you really needed me, I'd chuck it all aside and go with you. But as a physician, I think it is probably very important for you to reenter your old habitat and let the chips fall where they may. You need to relearn being Giles and if I go with you, 'Mark' might be too much on your mind. Just try not to forget me, hey? You have a habit of doing that, just wiping out the past, you know." She tousled his thick, dark hair affectionately.

"Never, not you. You're part of my soul, as essential to me as breathing. And now it's your turn, Jackie, to promise me something."

"Anything, love. Anything."

"You don't know this Giles Hafferty fellow. You may hate his guts. I may, too, but I guess I'll be stuck with him."

"Don't talk nonsense," she interrupted.

"Shhh, now. Let me finish. However it turns out, do just one thing for me. If I don't turn out to be what you want in life, don't be too bitter. Remember the good times."

Jackie's reply was slow in coming. It occurred to her that they were being a bit prematurely melodramatic. Everything could turn out fine and dandy. This fear, half apprehension and half intuition, *could* evaporate. But somehow she doubted it. At best, the moment was bittersweet. "Perhaps I'll drink this after all," she said, taking up the glass of brandy, then letting the liquid flow down her throat like mellow fire.

"Let's go to bed," he suggested. "You must be tired. Such a long and trying day."

Arms encircling each other's waists, they wandered slowly through the big house, checking all the lights and locks.

"I may get a cat," she said slowly.

"A *cat*?"

"Why not? Don't tell me you're not a cat person?"

He laughed at her. "I hadn't thought about it. Cats are all right, I suppose. I was just wondering why you thought of cats out of the blue."

"Well, you'll be leaving and I've gotten used to having someone around. There are always signs on the bulletin board at St. John's advertising free puppies and kittens. The hours I keep, a dog would get lonely. But cats are more independent and self-sufficient."

"Replaced by a cat," he said dourly.

They started the path up the stairs, stopping on every other step to kiss. Mark's mouth was so warm and sweet she felt in danger of drowning in her own runaway sensations.

"I wouldn't say 'replaced,' " she said breathlessly after pulling away from him and advancing one more step. "If and when you come back, I wouldn't plan on getting rid of the cat. You'd have to learn to live together."

"Kiss me again. I think this set of stairs gets longer every night."

"Builds anticipation."

"Well, I'm 'anticipated' to my limit." With a sudden move, he scooped her up in his arms and carried her the rest of the way to the bedroom. By the time he had removed his clothing and joined her on the bed, she had freed herself of the pink robe. He nuzzled her shoulders, moving the narrow straps of the gown aside, and the filmy confection of lace and ribbon fell away to expose her creamy breasts. She pulled his dark head against her and gloried in the magic of his lips and hot, velvet tongue as they caressed the soft mounds and their tautly erect tips.

They took a long time with each other, savoring to the fullest the sweet game of building a fire, then retreating from it. Then, unable to prolong the moments of ecstasy any longer, she moved with him once more to that place where pain and pleasure are exquisitely inseparable. She dug her nails into his back, mindless in her passion, yet she heard herself call his name—the name she had given him—over and over again. The sound of her voice seemed to come to her from a great distance, as through a narrow tunnel, a tunnel intense with white heat.

As he often did when passion was spent, Mark laughed and moved tender, butterfly kisses across her face. When his lips touched her long, thick lashes, they encountered tears. Without shame, his own began to flow. They lay together, bodies lightly touching, laughing and crying together. Neither of them was able to tell where his tears began or hers ended.

"Whose name will you call when we make love again?" he whispered, the words falling gently from his lips.

She did not answer, but let her head find its favorite nest between his arm and shoulder. This could be the beginning of the end, she thought. Or, viewing it optimistically, the beginning of a new beginning. Either way, it would never be the same again. Undoubtedly they would lie together again, thigh against thigh, mouth against mouth, but he would never be Mark again. Really, he wasn't now. Mark P. Dolan was of the past. But it didn't hurt to pretend, just this one last time.

"I believe I'll call the office and have them reschedule my morning appointments," she told him over breakfast the next morning. "That will give us a few more hours together, until they come to take you away."

"You make that sound so ominous," he protested with a laugh. "As if they were going to drag me off to the funny farm or a federal penitentiary."

She made a mocking face and shrugged her shoulders. "Who knows? You might be having delusions."

"We'll see. If I am, I'll try to get Napoleon's autograph for you while I'm being treated. How's that?"

"You're so good to me."

He cupped her chin with his hand and looked lovingly into her eyes. "Seriously, Jackie, I think we'll both be better off if you go on to work. I have some things I need to do besides the finishing touches in here." He surveyed the kitchen he had created, a room that now possessed beauty, dignity, and warmth. "We're in danger of making something bigger out of this than it is. Nothing could top the farewell scene last night, and I'll only be gone for a short while. And I'll be calling you daily in the interim."

"I suppose you're right," she agreed reluctantly. "I keep wanting to hang on to Jackie and Mark until the last possible moment. Trouble is, it's already past."

Kisses flavored the coffee, juice, butter, and jelly as they finished their breakfast. When Jackie went back to her room and came down again, neatly groomed in office attire, Mark was not in the kitchen. Since the truck was there, she knew he was in the house somewhere, but she did not look for him. She held her back unnaturally straight as she walked to the garage, started her car, and backed out. Mark—*Giles*—had been right. There was nothing to be gained by prolonging good-byes.

Luckily, her day was a busy one. Often she needed to have more leisure time; this day, however, time to sit and think was something she most definitely did *not* need.

When she got home, it was well past dark. No one had turned on the lights so that they beamed a welcoming out to her. No one had popped a casserole into the oven so that her nostrils were assailed with the aroma of good, hot food. Tears of self-pity welled up in her eyes. She told herself she was being silly, but the tears were there all the same.

She flipped on the kitchen light, looked about at the few last touches Mark had added, and wondered how long it would take for her to remember that wasn't his name anymore. It was a good kitchen now. One to live in, love in, cook for your friends and family in. But, God, it was big when only one rather thin young woman stood in its center all alone. Suddenly she became aware of strange sounds and began to look about in the corners. A box sat to one side of the refrigerator, just out of sight. She approached it suspiciously. The sides of the box were rather tall, certainly tall enough to foil the small kitten's chances of getting out.

Jackie caught her breath sharply and kneeled down beside the little creature. It was a dark, nearly bluish gray, except for part of its face, a strip down the chest, and four tiny paws which were all snowy white. Its face was heart-shaped and piquant, topped by sharply pointed ears. A note was taped to the side of the box. In Mark's handwriting, she read the short message. "This is Marcus, my wee surrogate. You two look out for each other. I'll call you late tonight, my love. Giles."

Giles, she thought. Maybe it was her imagination but the "G" looked a bit shaky, as if it wasn't sure it had the right to be placed upon the paper. The kitten's mewing noises increased. In fact, he sounded quite impatient and out of sorts. No wonder, she thought. He had been confined to that box since *he* had left. She lifted the tiny cat from the box and cradled it lightly against her blouse, stroking it gently and speaking words of reassurance. If Marcus minded the few tears that fell on his down-soft fur, he didn't let it show.

While she prepared their suppers, she let the kitten play about freely on the kitchen floor. He was such a dear, amusing little thing, poking his head curiously around all the corners and into open cabinet doors. He lapped up the milk gratefully and she wondered if she were spoiling him by warming his milk. Not that it really mattered. It was no big deal to pour a bit of milk in a pan and set it on the electric range. She ate her own sandwich without interest. Even filet mignon would have tasted like sawdust tonight.

She took a long, lazy bath in hot water steeped with fragrant bubbles. It didn't soothe her as much as she had hoped it would, but it did help some. After sprinkling herself liberally with baby powder, she put on the old white nightshirt, its fabric limp and soft. She then regarded the cat with a pensive air. He appeared to be viewing her in much the same way. "Marcus, I wonder if you're housebroken," she said aloud. "No, I suppose not. You're much too small to have learned anything yet. Well, then, let's take a trip outside. Tomorrow we'll have to have a serious discussion in regard to litter boxes, I suppose."

Outside in the cool night air, she kept a close eye on the cat as he bounced about trying to catch the shadows cast by the many trees and bushes. There were thousands of stars in the sky. Now it would be impossible to pick out the wishing star. For things to remain good when they changed—that had been *his* wish. And hers. She closed her eyes tightly for a moment, just as she had done so often as a little girl. She wished that all those stars were wishing stars and that they were combining their magic right now, at this moment. Her wish was not unlike a prayer.

"Hope I didn't wake you, love."

All those miles between them and yet his voice was like a caress to her.

"How's it going?"

There was a pause and she knew that he was shrugging his broad shoulders before he answered, as he so often did. "It's a strange feeling, Jackie. Some things are familiar, others quite alien. All the gaps aren't filled in. Maybe they never will be. But I think I would have known Mother even if she hadn't 'introduced' herself. And I knew the house here in Boston even better. I don't really *remember* it yet; still, I can go from room to room without faltering. It's uncanny."

"I suppose it would be. Hey, thanks for the kitchen and the cat."

He gave a joyous laugh that caused her heart to turn completely over. "Little Marcus? I hope you didn't mind me naming him. It seemed to fit him somehow. And of course, there was an ulterior motive. I'm sort of hoping the name will remind you of me."

"As if I could forget."

"He isn't a fancy cat. No particular kind, but I suppose you've already figured that out. I was on my way to this place where they breed and sell Siamese, then a light snapped on inside my head and I turned right around and went the other way toward the animal shelter. I knew that's what my Jackie would want, to rescue some forsaken animal. And that's where I found Marcus. He's had his shots."

"You know me well. Regular bleedin' heart, ain't I?" she said softly.

"I'm not complaining. I wouldn't change you if I could, my love. God, how I miss you. You still think it's best I go it alone here for a while?"

"It's hard for me to say because I want to be with you so, but I do think it's best for now. Call me often; write me. Give it three or four weeks. That will put you over that critical three-month posttrauma period."

"And then?"

"And then, we'll play it by ear."

"Let's hope the tune's pleasant. It's late. I'll let you sleep." After giving her his telephone number in the house in Boston, he said, "Good night, Jacqueline Marie. Sleep well. I love you."

"I love you, too, Giles." She spoke that name for the first time, feeling quite bashful in doing so. He was her love and yet he was also a stranger.

She emptied out an old wicker basket, lined it with soft, worn towels, and put Marcus in it. Then she set the basket in the corner of her room where she could hear him if he began to make suspicious noises in the night. However, before either of them had gotten a wink of sleep, the tiny cat tried to climb up the silken counterpane on her bed. Instead of discouraging him, she lifted him up with a helping hand. There was some comfort in having the warm ball of fur nestled contentedly nearby.

Time took on a surreal quality for Jackie. Hours drifted into days, days into weeks. She still took an interest, of course, in her work, which, as always kept her busy. What free time she did have, kind Marge tried to fill.

"You'd make a good tour director," Jackie complained affectionately once after Marge had carefully mapped out an entire weekend for her.

"How's What's-His-Face doing now?" Marge dared to ask. "Gads, Giles Hafferty. I can't get over that, though I should have known. Even when we knew him, he certainly fit no humble mold."

"He calls often. And believe it or not, he writes. Long and loving letters."

"Then he must be in love," Marge quipped. "Most men I know loathe personal letter writing. Rich for instance. We were apart once when we were engaged, for nearly three months. I wrote every day and I got two letters from him the entire time. And one was only a postcard. How affectionate and erotic can you get on a postcard? I tell you, Jackie, I was hurt. I was on the verge of breaking the engagement. Couldn't stand the thought of marrying such a lout."

"I remember when that was going on," Jackie said with a laugh. "You came by my apartment one day, all tears and righteous indignation. Rich was due home the next day and you were determined to break the engagement. So I dropped by *your* place after classes the next day, all ready to mumble cheery platitudes, and there you were, radiant and happy."

"Because he was home and that made all the difference," Marge replied with a dreamy, romantic look on her face.

"Uh-huh, Marge. A room full of roses and a diamond ring the size of a cowbell put forth some pretty convincing arguments."

Marge only gave a little giggle. "But we're straying from the point—how is his memory?"

"He tells me it's coming back more strongly all the time. There are great stretches of time he can recall well, and other stretches he still can't remember at all. Chances are, Marge, he'll never remember the events directly surrounding the accident; that limited type of permanent amnesia is fairly common. That shouldn't be a real problem, though, if he can get back the rest of it."

"Maybe I shouldn't ask, but is he coming back?"

Jackie shifted her shoulders slightly. "Don't be afraid, Marge. If Giles and I have learned anything these few weeks apart, it's that we are truly in love with each other. I don't know what we'll work out, or when, or how. But we will work something out. All along I knew this was no casual affair. He holds my heart."

"Think of it," Marge said, stretching her rather short legs lazily, "all that money and power. You'll never have to work again."

Jackie gave her a curious look. "Don't be silly, Marge. When I quit practicing medicine, I'll quit breathing."

"Have you talked to *him*—to Giles—about that?"

"Not really. Our conversations consist of generalities and endearments. I must admit that I sometimes have an odd little feeling that he isn't telling me everything. But I *do* trust him, so I suppose there's a good reason for the little evasions. His month is almost up, so we'll see each other soon. Here or there."

No one gave her the magazine or alluded to it in any way. Although it was a nationally known weekly news magazine, she did not subscribe to it. Its nearest rival crossed her desk each Wednesday, was quickly read, and sent to the waiting room. No, her friends and colleagues were all much too kind to bring it up.

She saw it herself while grocery shopping. The cover glared at her brightly from among all the other publications in the magazine rack. Even without the red and gold bordering to call attention to the face, she would have noticed that cover. The black, almost ebony hair and that brilliant, rakish smile were so familiar. Heart beating wildly, she snatched a copy of the magazine from the shelf and put it in her cart. His face continued to look up at her from amid the loaf of bread and the celery stalks. Giles Hafferty. He looked exactly like a man who was quite accustomed to having what he wanted, when he wanted, and, most surely, *whom* he wanted.

Jackie filled the cart haphazardly after that. She was dying to get home and read that magazine, being much too reserved to stand in the aisle of the store trying to learn about the man who was her lover.

She was controlled enough to put away the things that required refrigeration and considerate enough to give Marcus his dinner before she indulged her curiosity.

The magazine was a reputable one, and Jackie believed what she read. She most certainly, however, did not like what she read. No wonder Mark—*Giles*—had seemed evasive.

Her eyes scanned the pages rapidly. How could she have escaped hearing of this man? All the companies he controlled, all the publicity he had received. That's what comes, my dear, of being so absorbed in medicine, she chided herself. It all made quite an interesting article. So rich, so powerful, so handsome . . . and he had nearly lost it all when a blow on the head in a strange city and state had taken his memory.

Giles Hafferty had flown to Mississippi to attend a lavish party given on a riverboat by the Montgomerys. She had heard of the Montgomerys. They were notorious for their jet-setting lives, for the frequent and generally wild parties they threw. Just an intimate little get-together with a few good friends, say three or four hundred, and to the devil with the cost. Not a southerner in the bunch of them, and they had elected to throw a dinner party and dance in Biloxi. According to the story, Giles Hafferty had walked out in the middle of the party. He had told some friends he was going after a particular brand of scotch the host had not provided and that he would be back quickly. He had not rented a car, so they assumed he had taken a taxi. When asked if anyone had become concerned when he had not return, some of the guests explained that a certain young woman had disappeared about the same time. A certain young *married* woman who had had her eye on the attractive Hafton heir for quite some time. Her much older, very jealous husband had stalked about irately all evening and was even heard to make comments about what he'd like to do to that young so-and-so.

Thus, when Giles's absence was prolonged, this information was relayed to his family and closest friends and associates, who then assumed he was "laying low" for a while. No one had thought to ask the young woman and her husband. Apparently they should have. Being in the early stages of pregnancy and quite nauseous, she had returned home. Giles's ring and watch had since shown up in a pawnshop. The authorities seemed to assume there had been no personal motives in the attack on Giles, that muggers had spotted an obviously well-heeled man out alone in a bad neighborhood and had thus relieved him of his possessions. They supposed the muggers had exchanged clothing with him because they thought a drunk lying in the gutter would attract less attention than a naked man.

The story made it quite clear that Giles, though innocent in this particular instance, had a long-standing history of such escapades with women. It was not unusual for him to disappear at times for a cooling-off period.

Shaking her head, she looked back at the cover again,

hoping the magazine had magically turned into one of those tabloid scandal sheets. But no, staid and staunch, widely read and known through the world for accuracy, the name of the publication stared back at her.

Giles was a jet-setter, a womanizer, a man reputed to be always willing to take a chance with a fast boat, a fast car, a fast woman. Even allowing some margin for journalistic exaggeration, Jackie knew some truth was there. He was not exactly her preconceived notion of a noble soul.

The telephone rang. She knew, even before his voice came through the receiver, that it was Giles.

"How's my sweetheart?" he asked lightly. "You can't imagine how I look forward to hearing that magnolia-blossom accent across all these miles."

"I'm fine, Giles. And you?" She was well aware that her voice had a strangled quality. Giles chatted breezily for a while. Her replies were laconic. Being casual was not a possibility for Jackie at the moment.

"Jackie, what's wrong?" he asked at last.

"Nothing. I'm fine. Maybe I'm just a bit tired." Again the hollow, haunting sounds.

"Damn and blast it all anyway. You've seen that magazine, haven't you?"

For a brief moment, during which her heart was in her throat, she waited with a grain of hope. She waited for him to tell her it was a pack of lies, all pure fabrication. She waited in vain.

"You don't know, my love, how sorry I am that you had to find out this way."

"I'm sorry, too. It would have been easier if you had leveled with me."

"I know. I've been struggling with finding a way. Jackie, I have to see you."

"Then jet on down, honey. I'll see if I can rent a riverboat in your honor."

All the fury she had been pushing down rose up and would not be denied. Afraid of saying even more, she hung up the telephone. She didn't slam it or bang it; she merely set it to rest easily. When it rang again, she did not answer it. After a while it did not ring anymore.

She hunted up the cat and went to bed. Knowing she would not sleep, she still wanted to be alone in the darkness. "I suppose I'd confuse you if I changed your name now, Marcus," she said softly as she petted the soft fur.

The objective side of her knew she should reserve judgment and not be so hurt and angry until she had talked to Giles in person. But the other side of her prevailed. She found herself wondering how long he had known these things, if his amnesia had ever truly been that deep after the first few days. He *was* amnesiac at first, she'd stake her professional reputation on that. But afterwards, she had become so quickly and thoroughly enthralled with him that her "professional opinion" might have been swayed by personal emotions.

How long, how long? she wondered. How long had he known who he was and what he was and kept it from her? How long had it been a lark, the rich playboy putting on an injured act and letting himself be seduced by the serious-minded lady doctor? The wondering was like a grieving. She tried to reason with herself and stop it, but she could not. She could not help feeling Mark—*Giles*—had betrayed her in some fashion. And the hurt of the betrayal was deep, wide, and set her apart from all she had loved.

Physician, heal thyself, she thought ironically as she

lay alone in the bed she had shared with *him*. Able to stand it no more, she moved herself and Marcus to an empty bedroom at the end of the hall. It wasn't a very nice room, but it did have one great advantage: there were no memories of Giles there. Sleep did come but it was troubled with very disturbing dreams.

Chapter Seven

When Jackie arrived home the next evening, Giles was there. She wasn't surprised. She could hang up the telephone and refuse to answer letters. But face-to-face she could not resist him and he knew that.

His dark eyes were compelling, pleading, and his smile spoke of love. In a moment, she crossed the room and was in his arms, her tears soaking the fine fabric of his shirt.

"No wonder you left DePaulo's old clothes behind," she finally said shakily. "You look marvelous, Giles. Being rich becomes you."

"Does it? I suppose it's a habit to which one could easily take hold. Are you going to talk to me now, darling? Not about clothes or weather or neurology. About us."

They sat on the shabby sofa in the front room, Jackie's head comfortably resting against his shoulder. "I'm sorry I blew up last night. It was a very adolescent way to behave."

"Don't apologize. I admit to being guarded with the truth. The past month has been like an avalanche—just as you said it would be. The memories have cascaded

142

past my consciousness so fast it makes me dizzy. Most of it is back now. I've been less than truthful with you about what's been going on in Massachusetts because I feared your reaction. I can see now that was stupid. Ask me anything you want, I'll tell you all I can. But, please, whatever else you think or do, keep remembering I love you."

Jackie nodded her understanding. "Just tell me how it happened for you, tell it your way. I don't know what to ask you."

"When I was completely amnesiac, you were all the world I knew, all I wanted. I was—*am*—completely in love with you. When the first memories began to stir, when I had some inkling of what my past life had been like, I felt very uneasy. That life isn't compatible with your life. You live to serve, to help, to make the world a better place. I don't know that I've ever done a useful thing, Jackie. Believe me, I take no pride in saying that."

"Don't you work awfully hard?" she asked. "I mean, all those big companies to run . . ."

He stroked her hair affectionately. "I show up at the more important stockholders' meetings and cast my vote. My father died only a few years ago, but he didn't do anything either. He and Mother were always out on the yacht, or flying to the Riviera, throwing parties. It was our way of life and I went right along with it. It's all I've ever known."

"I can't believe you're *bad*," she said. Her voice was very soft and she felt somehow childish. "You're just *not*."

"No, I don't think I am either. Just a trifle too rich, too spoiled. Our life-styles and backgrounds are so totally different. As you observed yourself when we were trying to figure out who I was, I'm not addicted to alcohol or drugs. The women . . ." He smiled down at her but she could not accurately read his expression. "Poor excuse, I guess, but I've never seduced a woman. When they ran after me, I let myself be caught. A weakness, I suppose."

It was with a certain amount of pain that Jackie recalled the night of the thunderstorm when they had first made love. He hadn't seduced her. If fact, he had tried to talk her out of it, but when she caught him, he hadn't run away.

He seemed to know what she was thinking and he drew her more closely against him. "None of them ever really mattered, Jackie. Not until you. Can you believe that?"

Looking up into his beloved face, she believed him. Heaven only knew what would happen between them, but there was love. She touched his chin with her fingertips almost shyly. "I had a terrible night last night. I kept imagining that you pretended the amnesia, that you made a fool of me as a woman and as a doctor.."

"You still think that?"

"No."

"Good. The story that was in the magazine—I don't remember those things. I remember coming to Mississippi and going to that stupid party. Right now, however, I don't remember leaving the riverboat or anything after that point, until I woke up and saw your sweet face."

"So where do we go from here?"

"Come with me to Boston for a while."

"I can't . . ."

"Shhh, just listen," he said, lightly putting a finger on her lips. "*Before* I remembered, I hated the feelings of inadequacy, hated the idea that you had to take care of me. Now all that is reversed. I can take care of you in a way you've never dreamed possible. You won't have to fool with restoring this house bit by bit anymore. Anything you want, anytime, anyway. It's that simple. So many nights I've seen you tired, weary to the bone. You won't have to work like that now."

"Giles, I don't *have* to work like that. I thought you understood. Are you asking me to give up medicine?"

"No, of course not, love." His voice was as soothing and sweet as honey. "I'm sure you'll want to have an office, see some patients now and then."

"A rich woman's hobby. Seeing a few socialites with migraine headaches in my spare time."

"Jackie, rich people can be genuinely ill and need medical help. The poor don't have a patent on disease or pain."

She stood up and walked to the wide window. "What is it you have in mind, then?"

"I'm not asking you to come tonight. And not forever. Take care of the most immediate things here, then come see how things are in the East. A few weeks' vacation. We'll work out the details there. It's not entirely an ugly world there, Jackie. People are just people wherever they are. Hopping about all over the world at a moment's whim—it can be fun. You deserve a vacation. Won't you give it a try?"

"I have so many patients, so many obligations . . ." Her voice trailed off lamely.

"And you have a whole troop of colleagues who owe you favors. Please?"

He was standing right behind her, his hands lightly on her shoulders. She knew she wanted to be with him. She had missed him this past month more than she would have ever believed it possible for her to miss anyone.

"Don't be stubborn, sweetheart. I lived here with you awhile. You come with me awhile. Fair enough?"

When she answered him, her voice was strong and steady. "Okay. Give me a couple of weeks to get things arranged here, then Marcus and I will come to Boston and give it a whirl."

"That's my Jackie, that's my love." She let herself be held and comforted. It was a curious thing, she thought, that she needed comfort at a time that was the beginning of a new life for them. An uneasy thought occurred to her that perhaps she just might be wanting to have it all her way. Only she couldn't. Clinging to him like a woman in danger of drowning, she let her worries fade in the wake of their returning passion.

Once she had told him that the future would have to take care of itself. It was still that way.

"Yeah, sure, I'll see them for you," Pitillo said with a grin. "I owe you that and a million things more. What a stroke of luck, kid. Your anonymous patient ends up being a tycoon who begs you to come to the city and marry him. It's like a fairy tale."

Jackie smiled and went along with his good-natured kidding. Similar comments were plentiful these days. She couldn't really blame people for their interest. The story definitely had a lot of Cinderella appeal. The trouble was, she thought wryly, she rather enjoyed being the poor Cinderella. Certain aspects of it, anyway.

Ten days after Giles's visit, Jackie was ready for departure. To spare Marcus the misery of traveling in a plane's baggage compartment, she decided to drive. With autumn moving into full swing, she should encounter some lovely scenery.

On the long drive, she had a good deal of time to think. Her moods underwent rapid changes. For a few miles, she would be quite optimistic and certain that she and Giles would work things out. A few miles more and the doubts would seize her. They had so many differences now. She talked to Marcus about the situation, and although he was a very attentive audience, his suggestions weren't in the least helpful.

Her arrival at the Hafferty house was not exactly what she had expected. In the first place, "house" was an understatement. Jackie herself had a big house, but *this* place was beyond belief. Created when craftmanship was king, the huge brownstone mansion had been meticulously maintained. The rooms, with their high ceilings, would have accommodated a giant easily, and all the woodwork, archways, and hearths were intricately carved and detailed.

Carrying Marcus's case with one hand and her handbag with the other, she felt dwarfed as soon as she entered the house. For a brief moment, she stood there alone in her navy and white ensemble and attempted to suppress the urge to flee. That urge ended when Giles came flying down the palatial stairs two at a time. He wore beige slacks, a brown polo shirt, and a big, welcoming grin. He picked her up, Marcus and all, and swung her around exuberantly until the loud meowing sounds of protest grew almost frantic.

"Sorry, wee Marcus," he said with a laugh, petting the cat through the bars of his box. "Only he's not so wee anymore, is he?" Not giving her a chance to answer, he kissed her vigorously.

"This must be Jacqueline, then," said a feminine voice.

Jackie pulled back from Giles and looked across the huge room to the lady who had just entered. She was slim, golden-haired, and elegant. At first glance, she appeared hardly older than Giles. Closer inspection, however, revealed a tautness to her skin that spoke of cosmetic surgery. Blushing slightly, Jackie admitted who she was. "And you're Giles's mother?" she ventured.

"That I am. Anne Hafferty, and I'm ever so pleased to meet you at last. Giles goes on and on about you for simply hours to anyone who will listen."

"Then you must have some awfully dull conversations," Jackie said with a laugh.

Anne proved to be all charm and hospitality. She quickly issued orders to the servants to have Jackie's car parked in the garage and to have her luggage carried in. British tea was then served in the white and gold room as they talked.

Anne said warmly, "I do want you to know how much I appreciate the help you gave Giles during his strange 'illness.' Without you, it's difficult to say what might have happened to him." She looked at Jackie appraisingly, then gave a tinkling laugh that resembled the rattling of the fine china cups and saucers. "I must admit that when he told me he was going to marry you, I thought he might be doing it out of sheer gratitude. Now I know better." With carefully controlled grace, she turned her smile toward her son. "She's exquisite, Giles."

"Of course. Classic beauty beyond compare. Look at those high cheekbones, at those exotic eyes."

"Hey, that's enough," Jackie protested. "You're embarrassing me."

After they had all talked for a while, Jackie and Marcus were shown to their quarters to freshen up before dinner. After the excellent dinner, Anne excused herself, and Giles and Jackie spent the rest of the evening alone. He showed her through the beautiful house, telling her bits of its history as they went.

"This is nice," she commented once. "Now it sounds silly, but I had expected to enter Boston with a bang. I thought you'd be having some gala, lavish party."

"Disappointed?"

There was no hesitation in her denial. "Being alone with you is one of my favorite pastimes."

He grinned and hugged her affectionately. "Just wait till tomorrow night. We're having a few people in to meet you."

"How few is 'a few'?"

He shrugged nonchalantly. "Two hundred or so."

"Good grief."

"You'll survive. Hope you don't mind that I told Mother I'm going to marry you. I realize there's been no official, formal proposal, but . . ."

"But, what?" she asked, looking up at him with adoring eyes.

"You *are* going to marry me, aren't you?"

"Try to get out of it, boy. You see, this was the plan all along. I really knew who you were. I figured if I played my cards right and made you properly grateful . . ."

"It worked."

Their playful kisses grew more intense and Giles escorted her up to her suite of rooms where he made love to her quite thoroughly in the wide, antique Queen Anne bed.

This wasn't so bad after all, Jackie thought before she drifted off to sleep.

* * *

The next evening altered her optimistic point of view considerably. The music, food, drinks, and general ambience were all excessive. She was introduced to so many people she felt almost dizzy. They all merged into a blur so that, finally, she could not tell one from another.

She wore one of her favorite dresses, a simply cut mauve. She had always felt confident and attractive in the dress, until tonight. Among all the designer outfits and custom-made items, she felt almost gauche.

"So you're Giles's fiancée. I wish you luck in taming that man—you'll need it."

"Such a pretty woman, darling. So fresh and unspoiled."

"You're a neurologist? How simply fascinating. I think I saw fourteen neurologists until I finally gave up and started seeing a shrink."

"I suppose you'll live here in the East somewhere when you're married. God, I can't imagine Giles in Mississippi. I mean, what is there to Mississippi? Spanish moss and smelly wharfs. No cultural atmosphere really."

"I *do* just love your accent, dear. Tell me, did it take much practice?"

The voices were brittle, high, staccato, and they seemed to be closing in on her. Clouds of smoke billowed about their faces. Jackie smiled a lot and talked a lot. When it was all over, she was not sure what she had said.

"I don't think I'll remember any of them," she admitted to Giles later. "It's going to be dreadfully embarrassing when I meet them again because I know I won't recognize anybody."

"Don't worry about it," he said, stretching out lazily like a big cat across the bed. The little gray cat promptly sat on his chest and looked him right in the eye. "Quit staring, Marcus, or I'll take you back to the animal shelter. Anyway, darling, they'll all know you. They sure think you're a pretty thing."

"Yes, I'm sure I made a great impression in my forty-dollar dress. Gracious, Giles, I bet your *socks* cost more than that."

He made a funny face at her, then kissed the pulse point of her wrist. "On *you*, anything looks as if cost a million."

A giggle bubbled up inside Jackie and overflowed. "Some woman asked me where I got my 'devastating frock.' I told her the truth, that it came from a store in a mall in Biloxi. I don't think she believed me. She's the one who threw away her Gucci."

"Pardon?"

" 'Dahling, the past year or so, I was positively mad for Gucci. You know how it is. Well, I simply had to have the *first* of anything he did. Everything, and I mean everything, I had was Gucci. Then, unaccountably, I sickened. Couldn't stand anything Gucci anymore. And when something is passé with me, it's passé. So I threw it all out. Just tore through the closets and drawers one morning and cleared it all out. Not a Gucci label or signature on the premises. Yet who knows what time will bring, or the next season? It may be Gucci for me again. Just think of starting all over.' "

Jackie did a good job mimicking the stilted eastern accent and Giles was helpless with laughter by the time she was finished. "You're cruel, Jacqueline," he said. "Funny but cruel."

"Not so. I acted very polite and interested. But she sounded so serious about it, as if clothes were her whole world."

After she had made the comment, it occurred to her that it was very likely the lady's wardrobe was a major portion of her world. But she really didn't brood on the subject. She was here with Giles and that was what mattered. She had to be patient and fair and give herself a chance to get used to all this.

"What's on for today?" she asked, nibbling at the sweet roll that had been served to her on an elegant tray complete with a rosebud in a crystal vase. The life of the idle rich, she mused. No more too-black toast quickly stuffed down before running out the door.

"How about a tour around Boston, with an eye out for concerns of family interest? Look at it well, for you'll be mistress of all you survey. Thursday I have us scheduled to leave on a cruise to Nausau; won't be gone over a week. In fact, if the cruise is boring, we can cut it short and fly back. The Holdens are having some colossal dinner party. And I have some other events in store that should convince you this sort of life isn't totally bad."

"Like what?" she asked warily.

"A fashion show in Paris, a sports-car race in Italy, lots of things. I have a mountain chalet reserved in the Alps—thought you might want to see where the Swiss bank accounts are located. I'm hoping to appeal to your mercenary side in all this."

"All that planned for me? You shouldn't have. I'd certainly be content to hang around Boston and count the beans. Just as long as you're around too. Besides, I'll only be here two to three weeks, then I have to go back and see to my practice, my office."

"To close or to resume?" he asked lightly, although she suspected he did not regard it lightly.

"That depends," she said, patting his hand. "I'll have to resume for a while because I have patients scheduled. If we decide I should relocate here, then I'll close, but it will take awhile to arrange."

"Anything you say. As long as you keep an open mind."

"Oh, you're making that easy for me." She smiled at him as the uniformed maid moved silently and efficiently to take their plates and refill their coffee cups. "I'll probably never be cheerful about doing my own cooking again. I must admit, though, something about it makes me feel lazy and slothful."

He laughed at her indulgently. "Just relax and enjoy it. If anyone has ever earned the right to be a bit lazy and slothful, it's my favorite doctor."

The next few days descended and passed with the dizzying speed of a whirlwind. Bright and early the next morning, Giles started by giving her a tour of his hometown.

"Is there anything in Boston the Haffertys don't have a hand in?" Jackie asked. The tour of the historic city had caused her feet, clad in chic though uncomfortable shoes, to ache and her mind to whirl.

"Not much," he said with a pleased laugh.

As they walked along the street lined with old houses, their feet caused the fallen leaves to rustle and crackle.

"How many people work for your companies, directly or indirectly?"

He looked at her in surprise. "Why, I haven't any idea."

"That one place you showed me, a sort of subsidiary of Marchand Oil . . . weren't they involved in some sort of lawsuit awhile back? Something about dumping potentially dangerous chemicals in the waterways."

"Oh, could be. I suppose the attorneys handled all that. It must have been settled out of court, though. Surely I would know of an actual court case."

"Surely," she replied. If he noted the dry sarcasm in her manner, he did not comment upon it.

"I think you like the cruise."

"I think so, too, Giles."

And why wouldn't she, she thought, while they stood on the deck of the luxury liner looking up at the star-filled sky and out at the endless expanse of water. "But I do wish," she said wistfully, "that the energetic young activities director would take a leap over the side of the boat. I'm more into being with you than I am into group shuffleboard."

"Then I'll push her over for you. Anything to make you happy. Besides, being alone with you is just about one of my favorite activities, too."

"Just about?" she asked with feigned indignation.

He shrugged his shoulders and wrinkled his nose. "Well, really, I'm rather fond of group shuffleboard."

"Do tell? Then run up on deck and play awhile. I'll just go on back to my cabin and slip into something comfortable."

"Hmmm. Shuffleboard suddenly lost its appeal."

"Good. I can't stand competition."

Giles pulled Jackie into his arms and they stood closely pressed together, their slightly swaying bodies keeping time with the rhythm of the waves.

After the long and love-filled cruise, they stayed in a well-known luxury hotel in Nausau and ate in the finest restaurant. If Jackie so much as paused on the streets or in a marketplace to look at some object, Giles promptly bought it for her. He had been to the same area on several occasions and was surprisingly knowledgeable about native customs and folklore.

"How do you know all that?" she asked him lovingly when he had finished explaining the history of a dance form they had just witnessed. They had watched the colorful entertainment out in the open under the island's dark sky while they ate unrecognizable foods with unpronounceable name served by attractive young people in brilliant costume.

"Oh, I just get around and talk to lots of different people. It's an enjoyable experience, really. Soaking up local atmosphere, that is."

"Then you don't spend quite all your time partying, I see."

"Not quite all."

Although Jackie enjoyed the trip very much, there was one aspect of it she could have done without. Giles was recognized everywhere he went by other members of the "jet set" and they were always getting trapped into dinners and all sorts of things. Yet it occurred to her that she might be the only one who felt "trapped." These were his friends, the members of his social set. Sometimes, when their shallow, stilted conversations grated on her nerves, she thought she would scream, but she managed to clench her teeth and keep silent. If Giles enjoyed and liked these people, she could too. She would just have to give herself a chance to become accustomed to them. However, she found that this was more easily said than done. She was a woman who based a lot on first impressions. After all, she had loved Mark almost immediately, hadn't she? Or Giles, that is.

*　　*　　*

"There you are, Jackie. I looked all over that crazy house and couldn't find you. Aren't you chilly out here?"

Her bare shoulders, rising out of the lacy, ivory-colored blouse, were chilly. At present, she preferred the chill to the stale air of the Holdens' modern and spacious house.

"I'll go back in soon, Giles. It got a bit stuffy in there for me. In case you hadn't noticed, there's a rather thick blue haze in there. A person can get lung cancer by proxy. Reminds me of a hospital board and staff meeting. Only it seems to be going on much longer."

"I gather you're not exactly enjoying yourself."

She made an attempt at a smile. The results were rather poor and she was glad the visibility wasn't too great out on the lawn. "It's all right as parties go. I guess I'm just not a party person."

"They really like you, Jackie. Most of them. I'm always being told how sweet and fresh you are, what a good conversationalist."

At his words, Jackie felt somehow reproached. His friends liked her, why couldn't she relax and like them a bit? That wasn't what Giles had said, yet she had the feeling that was exactly what he meant.

"Don't pay attention to me, hon," she told him. "I'm just an old, dull stick in the mud. I didn't say I didn't like anyone. On a one-to-one basis, I'm sure I would. There's something, however, about a party atmosphere that freezes me up. Sorry."

He kissed her brow with obvious affection. "You don't ever have to apologize to me about anything. And I'll be glad to take you home if you're tired or uneasy."

"No, that's all right. You're enjoying it, so come on, I'm ready to go back."

Thus Jackie spent several more hours chatting animatedly with the rich. All in all, it probably wasn't any worse than the parties she got bullied into attending on occasion at home.

Home, she thought sadly. She wasn't even sure where that was now. Her house in Mississippi hadn't seemed much like home that month she spent there after Giles left. And the brownstone in Boston didn't exactly inspire feelings of home and hearth. There was not even much time to spend with Marcus. Giles kept her so busy going here and there that the small gray cat was neglected.

"You don't mind that the Barlows are going to Paris with us do you, Jackie?"

She did, though. She minded a lot. Instead of saying so, she smiled brightly and said, "Why, of course not."

"Good," he said, quite obviously pleased. "I thought Emily would be a great help to you at the fashion show. She really keeps up on such things."

"I know."

Giles's glance was keen and cutting. "Do I detect a note of sarcasm?"

"Only a touch. You surely don't want me to *buy* anything, do you? The cost of one item would be astronomical."

"So?"

Jackie let the conversation drop. But filthy rich or not, she was determined not to buy a bunch of unneeded Parisian fashions. She liked clothes and wanted to look her best, but there was no point in getting ridiculous about it. And without a doubt, the prices would be ridiculous.

When they were actually in Paris, she and Emily went to the fashion show alone. Giles and Emily's husband, Alex, had some obscure, though "extremely important" business matters to conduct. By their attire, Jackie imagined they were going to a gym to play handball or some such thing.

While nearly everyone else present ooohed and aaahed, Jackie squirmed, fidgeted, and wished the show would quit dragging on and on. The emaciated, highly made-up human mannequins strutted and struck poses with their hipbones at highly unlikely angles; it was a marvel, Jackie thought wryly, that they didn't throw something out of place permanently.

Just when she was beginning to be amused by her own errant train of thought, Emily nudged her and whispered, "That outfit there, the one that's coming out now—that's you."

Jackie looked up at the stage. A dark-haired girl was modeling a classic-looking ensemble of stark black and white. It was strikingly attractive, its style deceptively simple. She shook her head as she answered Emily, "That's the sort of dress the wearer has to dominate. I don't think I could do it."

"Oh, piffle and nonsense. As tall and thin as you are, you could wear anything. A different hairstyle, a bit more makeup, and *you*'d rule that dress. Better have Giles buy it for you."

"Really, Emily. We aren't even married yet."

"Might as well be. I've never seen him this way with a woman. But if you want to be stubborn about it, then buy it yourself. Doctors are loaded, aren't they?"

Jackie smiled and did not bother to reply; she didn't

really think a reply was expected. She looked over the price lists which had been discreetly placed at each table. One of those idiotic dresses, she thought, cost as much as a piece of medical equipment.

The next day, while she and Giles were getting ready to go out to lunch with Emily and Alex Barlow, the black and white dress was delivered. Jackie was dumbfounded.

"Giles, really, I can't accept this."

"Sure you can. Emily told me about it and I wanted you to have it."

"But now I'm the one who is danger of feeling like a gigolo—female style."

Giles promptly made fun of her: "I believe the proper term is—"

"Well, whatever," she said quickly.

"Really, Jackie. Just go try it on for me and shut up. You'll probably have to take it for fittings. They howled when I said I wanted it delivered first because that's not the way they do things."

"But for Hafferty they made an exception, right?"

"Something like that," he replied with his easy grin in place. "But I have to hold up my end of the bargain, too—it's not returnable. Goodness, woman, in Mississippi, you fed, clothed, and sheltered me. Can't I even buy you one dress?"

She knew she was defeated, but got in her last wry comment. "One dress, right. One dress which costs only slightly less than a car."

"You're a beautiful woman, Jacqueline. But stubborn."

Jackie tried on the dress for Giles. He marveled, then phoned the Barlows to come marvel along with him. She enjoyed some of the attention, yet she kept thinking of the thin, worn mats in the rehabilitation room at St. John's. They, and much more, could have been replaced for what she wore on her back.

"I think I want the red car to win. It's cute."

"What a way to describe a custom Ferrari. Your car at home, Jacqueline, is cute. That one out there executing turns at nearly two hundred miles an hour; that one's magnificent."

Jackie took another look through the binoculars and made an offhand gesture. "Looks cute to me," she said.

Giles appeared about ready to continue his good-natured hassling when a fellow whom everyone called Bink began telling them about *his* Ferraris. Jackie listened carefully as his tale unfolded. The unfortunate man only had two Ferraris at present. For a while, he hadn't been selling the old ones when he bought a new one. "Sentimental of me, I suppose," he remarked. Then he went on to say how he had been forced to sell because of limited garage facilities. He told vividly of each car's faults and virtues, his voice sounding like a lover remembering the romantic past.

I suppose it isn't all so different, Jackie thought, than doctors talking about their golf games or how many gallbladders they've removed. She had often heard that same note of fondness in their voices on such occasions.

The little journey to the Swiss Alps was nice. Jackie snapped picture after picture of the regal snow-crowned mountains. Once there, she made attempts at learning how to ski but spent most of her time picking herself up out of the snowbanks. Somewhat wistfully, she watched Giles winding down the slopes with seemingly effortless skill. He had been skiing, he had told her, since he was a small child. Often it seemed to Jackie there wasn't anything he hadn't seen, hadn't done, hadn't had.

They flew back to the States early the next week. Only a few days were left until Jackie had to return to Biloxi.

"We have to talk, you know, my love," Giles said one night after they had made love. His voice was warm and contented and he lay close against her.

"I know, Giles. But not tonight. Let's not spoil the mood with talk. Just hold me close and let me sleep."

And so he did.

When Giles announced that he had accepted an invitation for them to a party at the Kennerlys', Jackie was sharply hurt. She was leaving the next morning and had thought—assumed really—they would spend their last evening alone together.

And this party was a spur of the moment thing. They would have a fairly long ride to and from it, as the Kennerlys were not holding it at their town house but at their place on the Cape. To Jackie's relief, Giles did plan on the two of them driving there alone instead of getting in some chartered bus with a group of other guests.

"You can't put it off much longer, Jackie," he said gently on the way up.

"I know. And I suppose there's no real reason I can't practice neurology in or around Boston."

"You mean that?" His face lit up with a sunny joy that would have told her he loved her even if she hadn't already known it.

"Sure. You'll have to give me a few weeks to wind things down in Biloxi. The lease is about up on my office so that's no problem, but I'll need to do something with my house and get my regular patients referred to other doctors."

"And we'll be married as soon as you come back?"

"Most definitely. And don't try to get out of it."

"No way. As I'm sure you know, I couldn't feel more married to you than I do right now. It's simply a matter of making it legal. And, Jackie, about your house—don't be in a big hurry to get rid of it. We have some wonderful memories there. Maybe you could just hang on to it for a while?"

"Okay," she said, laughing and stretching her legs languidly. "I keep forgetting how rich you are."

"*We* are," Giles corrected.

"Whatever. Anyway, rich enough so that an extra house here and there is no big deal. Right?"

"Right."

"What kind of party is this tonight?"

"I don't really know. No particular kind, I guess. Just a bunch of friends getting together and talking. We won't have to stay late. I wasn't too keen on it, really, but Jeff Kennerly kept after me and after me. Made it real hard to say no."

Any resentment Jackie felt melted away at his words. Giles hadn't really wanted to attend the party; he just found it difficult to turn down a friend.

"No problem," she said lightly. "After a month or so, we'll have the rest of our lives."

"I'm so glad you can see it that way, that there's no real harm in my life."

The Kennerly party was much as the Holden party had been. At first, that is.

Subdued lighting, myriads of people dressed to the hilt, a steady beat of live music, and a continuous patter of voices, predominantly with distinctive accents that had been learned at home and/or in renowned universities.

When things first began to take on a different aspect, Jackie was bemused. There was an unnatural tension in the air. Or maybe the right word wasn't tension—more like a hilarity too highly sustained. A few of the people she had come to know were behaving differently, eyes bright and voices high and rapid. Backing away from a particularly obnoxious man, she sought out Giles.

"What's going on?" she asked. "Everyone seems to be drunk or something. And the evening is still early. Why, we haven't even had the promised clams yet."

Giles gave her a rather curious look, patted her hand, mumbled something about checking on the meal, and took off across the room. Careful not to get trapped in conversation with anyone, Jackie roamed around the room observing the Kennerly guests. The physician in her recognized their drug-induced state. That same part of her cursed herself for not recognizing it before. As a woman in love and trying to adapt to a new life-style, naiveté was understandable. In a physician, it wasn't even excusable. So where was it coming from, she wondered?

Once she began looking it wasn't hard to find. A long, elegantly arranged buffet was along one wall of the old Cape house. Silver bowls held various brightly colored "uppers." Artfully arranged among the amphetamines were the individual packets of cocaine along with just about any apparatus one might want to use with it. There was no attempt to disguise the illegal drugs. Everything was as boldly displayed as if it were innocent food and drink.

She was seized with indignant anger. Why shouldn't it be boldly displayed? These people had nothing to fear. They were so rich and powerful they felt immune to the law. And they probably were to a certain extent. Until something too public happened, like death. Her emotions were in a turmoil and she didn't know what to think or feel. She only knew she couldn't stay in this house any longer. Swiftly locating her handbag, she escaped the sights and sounds of the party. She had thought she would go sit in Giles's car until he was ready to go, but she found it was locked and she did not have a key. Jackie stayed in the parking area anyway. At last, he came looking for her.

His handsome face registered alarm and concern. "I've looked everywhere for you. Are you ill? You should have told me and I would have taken you home immediately. But you asked about the clams and I thought you were hungry and . . ."

Giles stopped talking and looked at her. For what seemed an eternity, their eyes were locked in a level gaze.

"Okay," he said somewhat wearily. "Something's wrong. Are you going to tell me about it?"

"Do I really have to?"

He gave the habitual shrug of his broad shoulders inside the custom-tailored jacket. "Listen, Jackie, I understand that what they're doing upsets you, but why are you so angry with *me*? I had no idea this would be going on here tonight. You know I don't use drugs. So what's your problem?"

Inexplicable tears filled her dark blue eyes and flowed freely down her face, making it difficult for her to answer. However, she ignored the tears as a nuisance and answered him directly. "I love you, Giles. More than I ever loved anyone. I think I'll always love you. But I can't live this way. I wanted to. Oh, I wanted to so badly, because I can't bear the thought of not being a part of your life."

His face grew grim and bitter. "As long as I hung around like a lapdog of some sort, our love was okay. Then it had to be *your* way, I had no choice. Now that I'm self-sufficient, you can't adapt to that. *Won't* adapt to it. Tell me, aren't you being a trifle narrow-minded?"

"I know you can't understand, Giles. Most men can't. I thought it was different between us, but that was before . . . before all this." A sweeping gesture of her arm and hand took in the beautiful old home on the picturesque Massachusetts coastline and the parking area jammed with automobiles of every expensive make.

Not speaking, he continued to look at her. His look was hard.

"I've spent long hours of my life trying to break people of drug or alcohol addiction. It does some horrible things to the central nervous system. I'm not preaching 'morals' or 'social reform,' I'm speaking as a doctor who has treated way too many cases of overdose and adverse reaction. But even without cocaine and other jolly drugs, I don't like this life, Giles. I tried. I tried to fool myself into thinking I could live this way, but I know now I can't, not even for you. If I submitted to it, you'd soon find I'm not me any longer. You fell in love with a dedicated woman doctor in Mississippi who led a rather dull life by your present standards. *Our* excitement consisted of eating popcorn and reading favorite passages to each other, and making wild, sweet love."

"We still do that," he said shortly.

"What, make love well together? Sure. But there has to be more than that to create a bond."

"You know, Jackie, that I can't settle down in Biloxi

and do odd jobs. I have way too many holdings and obligations here."

"Obligations, Giles?"

His dark eyes fell away from the line of her level gaze. "You're being stupid and stubborn. You haven't given things a fair chance here."

"Let's not wrangle around anymore. The way things have turned out, it's tragic that we ever had to meet and become involved. While it was going on, it had a fairy-tale quality. But not all fairy tales end 'happily ever after.' "

"Especially when the princess refuses to move to the castle," he said quite angrily.

"May I use your key, Giles? If you don't mind, I'd like to drive back into Boston alone. I want to be by myself. I'm sure you can find a way in with one of your 'friends.' "

He handed her the keys with some control, although she had the idea he really wanted to fling them in her face. She hadn't expected him to give in so easily. But she was already too hurt and confused for it to make much difference.

At first, she intended to sleep, then leave very early. Once inside the big brownstone, she changed her mind quickly. She knew she wouldn't sleep well anyway and it was probably best she leave without encountering Giles again. She didn't want to have to remember any more bitter words between them. Packing her bags quickly, she placed them in her little silvery car. Marcus seemed quite docile and sleepy and she risked placing him on a cushion in the passenger seat rather than confining him to his hated cage. She needed the comfort of his nearness.

She wrote a brief note and put it in Giles's room on his dresser. The note read: "I'm sorry. Try to understand. And remember my love. Jackie"

Putting his keys on top of the note, she left.

Chapter Eight

When she arrived home, Jackie saw why Giles had suggested she not sell the house. During her absence, strangers had moved swiftly and expertly. All of the rooms were restored—expensively, tastefully, and with historic accuracy. A gift from Giles, she assumed. Curious how little it impressed her. What he had done to the kitchen impressed her. The rest of it had no meaning.

Physically exhausted, she slept for a long, long time. Marcus stayed by her side all the while. Apparently he had not rested well on the trip and was relieved to be back in familiar surroundings.

She unpacked, did some laundry, and made a quick trip to the grocery store for supplies. She called her secretary at home to confirm she would be back at work Monday morning. There was a hollow within her heart; she did not know if she could ever fill it, but she was going to start trying. After calling Marge and a few other friends and colleagues to let them know she was back, she went back up to her room and, for a reason unknown to her, opened the closet door and looked at the black and white designer dress Giles had purchased in Paris.

Jerking it from the hanger, she placed it in a box. The dress was a symbol of feelings best forgotten. She knew a nurse at the hospital just her size who would be thrilled with the outfit.

In dealing with her friends and colleagues, Jackie employed a low-key but honest approach. She told them she and Giles had decided they had too many differences for things to work out between them. Her slightly remote manner when speaking of the subject discouraged more probing questions. Even Marge, good friend that she was, did not pry. She was extremely kind and supportive, making Jackie grateful for her friendship.

The days and nights progressed with a dreadful sameness. Ever and always the dedicated physician, Jackie became engrossed in her work. Those were the good times. The bad times came when she went home to her renovated mansion. Once she had not minded the solitude; now it was almost more than she could bear. Marcus passed his kittenhood and became more independent. He still curled on her bed at night, but he was very much his own cat. Everything had to be on his terms. *Like someone else I know,* Jackie thought wryly. *Independence is great, to a certain point, and then it has a lonely, hollow feel to it.*

To mask this hollowness, Jackie became increasingly submerged in her work. She was now quite glad when she was asked to fill in for other doctors or to work on some special hospital committee.

"Aren't you losing weight?" Dan Gallen, the hospital administrator, asked one day.

"I don't know," Jackie replied carelessly. "I haven't checked recently." She pulled at the waistband on her skirt and found it to be very loose. She didn't have time to eat much anymore. And to be honest, her appetite had gone the way of other things in her past.

"I'll take your shifts in ER this weekend, Vince."

The young doctor looked at her as if she'd gone stark raving mad. "Why on earth would you want to do that? It's my turn, and goodness knows, I have to ask you to do enough."

"Forget it," she said, somewhat embarrassed. "I guess I just didn't have anything else to do."

"Jackie, you got a problem you want to tell me about?"

Jackie got up to leave, but patted Vince's hand. "I have a problem, yes; but, no, I don't want to talk about it. Have fun in ER, Vince. And don't blame me when the going gets rough. I offered."

Later that day, when she dropped by the rehabilitation unit, she was greeted with a flurry of activity.

"What's all this?" she asked in amazement. New mats, fixtures, and equipment were being installed in the rehabilitation rooms. Some of the equipment was the newest and most sophisticated available; she noted with special pleasure the apparatus used for retraining aphasic patients.

"St. John's has finally been remembered," the administrator announced with a beam. "Very, very handsomely."

"Who on earth?" Jackie asked.

"Anonymous. Naturally, I'm curious. In the meantime, though, I'm just accepting."

The rest of the day was busy and Jackie gave the matter no more thought except to be pleased that someone had finally noticed how much was needed there. But reading the newspaper that night, she was confronted with an item about Giles:

Pictured above is Giles Hafferty, one of the country's most eligible young bachelors. On his arm at the Broadway premiere of a new play is Stephanie Gillam: young, blond, beautiful, and rich. This pair is frequently seen at many events and strong rumors buzz of an impending engagement announcement.

Pain shot through Jackie like the searing of a red-hot poker. It didn't take him long to replace me, she thought, as she threw the newspaper away with disgust. The anger was over in a flash. The pain remained. She suspected it would be around for a while. There was no way she could blame Giles. After all, she had certainly made it clear she didn't want him under the circumstances. It was more than understandable he would seek solace with someone who did not seem to regard him as worthless.

The controversy warred within her own heart and soul continuously. Giles Hafferty was not worthless and she knew it. *No* human being was worthless, least of all the man she loved. As a person, he was good and kind. Logically and objectively, Jackie could not blame him for his extravagant existence. She was honest and fair enough to realize her own existence would be judged extravagant by those in dire need. Sure, she did her share of "charity" work, but she also retained enough for a comfortable life-style. What did she expect the Haffertys to do? Give the oil company to the government of an impoverished nation?

Over and over the thoughts rolled through her consciousness. Yet she knew she could not give in. Although she had no objection to being rich, she wanted to lead a useful and productive life. And she wanted to be a good neurologist who gave help to anyone who needed it. Really, she thought sadly, "want" wasn't the right word. These urges were as basic as the ones to survive, to eat, to sleep . . . and to love. If she threw away her gifts, her needs, to live Giles's way, she would be betraying herself. After such a betrayal, she would have little left to offer Giles.

To keep depression at bay, she worked with even more fervor. She ate and slept even less. Always slender, she became nearly gaunt. Dark smudges appeared beneath her unique eyes and her high cheekbones showed more prominently as the flesh of her face diminished.

"You look awful," Marge said flatly.

"Gee, thanks," Jackie replied, trying to laugh it off.

Marge would not, however, dismiss it lightly. "Really, Jackie, you better start taking care of yourself."

"I'll be all right."

"You need some rest."

"I'll get some."

"When?"

"Later."

Jackie's parents came to visit during Christmas vacation and were shocked by her almost emaciated appearance. To soothe them, she promised she would take a few days off in January to go to a medical convention in New York.

Before she left for New York, she went by the hospital administrator's office to discuss a new policy at St. John's. Dan Gallen had to leave the room for a few minutes and she waited there for him. Feeling restless, she got up and roamed about the office. She wasn't an overly nosy person, just human. She glanced at the stack of letters and forms on the cluttered desk. One in particular caught her eye because she recognized the boldly scrawled signature. Bigelowe Enterprises had just made another sizable donation to St. John's Hospital, one which was also to remain anonymous to the staff as well as to the general public.

Jackie's being was flooded with a great tenderness. Mark had been the one to give so much to the rehabilitation center of the hospital. *Giles*, that is. How she wished that she could thank him. But she knew it was best to let the past alone.

While in New York City, she had an unexpected chance to thank him in person. Quite by chance the A.M.A. convention was being held in the same famous hotel as some gala social event attended by Giles Hafferty's set. Naturally he was present. So was Stephanie Gillam. She was clinging to his arm when they accidentally met Jackie in the lobby.

"How have you been?" Giles asked politely. His dark eyes, once so warm and loving, were unreadable.

"Fine. Busy, of course, but that's the way I like it."

"I know."

He did not comment on her marked weight loss. She thought it was possible he didn't even notice. Stephanie had enough curves to take a man's mind off the way any other woman might look.

"I want to thank you, Giles, for the donations to St. John's. They were more than generous and have made all the difference in the world."

"How did you know? I specifically requested that no one be told."

"No one told me. I suppose I should have guessed, but I didn't. I found out quite by accident. And I've mentioned it to no one else."

He gave his familiar shrug. "Glad it was useful. Everything else all right with you?" His look was searching, yet she had no idea for what he searched.

"Fine. Looks as if you're doing well."

At her comment, Stephanie flashed a brilliant smile. Giles neither admitted nor denied anything and the young woman's hold on his arm did not lessen. They exchanged a few more awkward sentences. Jackie intentionally left the impression she was doing very well in her old life in Biloxi. What else was there for her to do? Nothing had changed, not really. And Stephanie Gillam was eminently more suited to Giles. They had grown up the same way and would have no major adjustments to make to each other's habits.

Despite her cool reasoning, Jackie left New York before the convention was over. She didn't want to run the risk of meeting Giles again. Seeing him only reminded her of how much she loved him, even as a spoiled and jaded jet-setter. Not that it really mattered. He had a new love in his life now. She had no right to complain. And so she didn't; she just kept on aching.

The pace was especially hectic both at St. John's and at Jackie's private office. She had already seen more than an average number of patients in her office when she got called to St. John's for a consult on a new admission; she was needed to assess the extent of the patient's neurological impairment. Jackie had made the examination and had just finished dictating her findings when she dropped her pen. She bent over to pick it up, then rose rather quickly. Suddenly everything started swirling and she felt nauseous. She grabbed at the shelf, then everything went totally black.

When she woke up, she felt very foolish. Doctors,

nurses, orderlies—even a few curious patients—surrounded her from all angles. "Goodness," she said, giving a weak-sounding laugh, "how foolish of me. Just the sudden change in position, I guess. Don't look so alarmed, everyone. I'm quite all right."

"Like heck you're all right," said Dr. Pitillo firmly. "Take her somewhere and put her to bed. We're going to check this thing out here and now."

Jackie murmured protests but no one paid any attention to her. She had slipped from the position of doctor to patient and was thus subjected to an entirely different set of rules.

Only, she thought wryly, *real* patients were treated with a bit more kindness than she was. One by one, her learned colleagues visited her, clucked their tongues over the findings written on her chart, and then proceeded to give her lengthy lectures on how she, of all people, should know better than to let herself get in such a condition.

"I want up from this bed and out of here," she said angrily. "I have patients to see."

"Your patients are being taken care of by someone else, my dear," she was told. The intravenous tubes running from the bottles to her arms were intimidating even to a doctor. Jackie stayed in bed. She hadn't realized how very tired she was until she had been forced to quit. The blood transfusion and the daily injections of iron were the most humiliating procedures.

"Just look at that," her colleagues would say. "Your blood count is so low it's pathetic. Why, it's half what it should be. It's a wonder you hadn't passed out before. Ridiculous. If you couldn't or wouldn't eat, haven't you heard of vitamins and nutritive substances?"

Jackie had no reply that made any sense. She had

neglected her own health and that was that. If she tried to claim she had not, no one would believe her.

"You're taking a vacation, Jackie," said Dr. Kenneth Mann, chief of neurology at St. John's.

"I can't. I don't want to," she protested. "I have too much to do."

"You're taking a vacation," he repeated mildly.

Faced with his insistence, Jackie became indignant. "I really don't see how you can force me to do so. I'm an admitting physician at St. John's but I'm not on the hospital payroll."

Kenneth narrowed his eyes and scowled at her. "Maybe I can't 'force' you to, but I certainly can make it rough on you if you refuse to. *Dr.* Spencer, right now you present a very real danger to your patients. Do you want to risk passing out again? Perhaps in the middle of a spinal tap or some other delicate procedure? You are to take a month off . . ."

"I took time off when I went to Boston . . ." she argued feebly.

"You were even owed that in overtime. This is your vacation time, Jackie. Do it. As I started to say before you so rudely interrupted me, it will take a month to rebuild your strength and hemoglobin and iron content. Go somewhere away from things—rest, read, eat, relax. Gain weight. You used to round out things so nicely, and now . . ." He gave a regretful sigh and Jackie threw a wadded-up tissue at him.

She did, however, quit arguing. Although she definitely did not want time off to do nothing, she realized she had to submit to the idea of the vacation. Her behavior had not been very smart. She had abused her body. Now she had to give it time to heal and replenish itself.

*   *   *

For two weeks, she visited her parents. They indulged her and she submitted without protest. They let her sleep late, coaxed her to go to bed early, and prepared veritable banquets of rich, calorie-lean foods. When the boredom grew too great, she got out her old bicycle, hosed it off, and went for long rides along country roads. The cold winter air and good food combined to place roses on her cheeks and a bit of needed padding in strategic areas.

"You're still in love with that man, aren't you?" her mother asked gently one day.

"I suppose I'll always be in love with *that* man," Jackie replied honestly, "but it's just one of those things that couldn't be."

"Nonsense. When love exists, there's a way."

Jackie gave a deep sigh of exasperation. Mothers never thought their offspring had any sense, even if they were thirty-year-old neurologists. "It's all beside the point, Mother. He's already found someone else."

Helen Spencer raised her eyebrows and looked at Jackie skeptically. "Have you been in touch with him? Do you know that definitely?"

"Stephanie Gillam. A charming little postdebutante," said Jackie, unable to keep the bitterness from her voice.

"Ah-hah," Mother announced trimphantly. "Then you don't know as much as you think you do. Whether you wanted me to or not, I've kept rather close track of that young man. Anyone who has such a hold on my daughter's affection elicits my curiosity."

"Sure you're not just hoping for a rich son-in-law? If so, forget it."

"That really wasn't the point, dear, as I'm sure you know quite well. Although trips to Acapulco and the

Caribbean for little presents now and then *would* be nice."

Jackie knew her mother was kidding, but she shot her a murderous glance nevertheless. The older woman was unperturbed.

"The Gillam girl is marrying someone else, Jackie. A Wicklein or Wickliffe or something like that. Someone with gobs of money."

"They *all* have gobs of money, Mother. You wouldn't believe the money they have. But are you positive about Stephanie? I mean, the rumors were so strong. And even discounting that, I *saw* them together in New York. She was draped all over him like ivy around a tree trunk."

Helen Spencer's smile was smug. "I'm sure."

"Hmmm. Then it must be Alan Wickliffe. They're into steel."

"I do believe that was the name. Anyway, the engagement has been formally announced. Early spring, I do believe."

"Anything else you 'do believe,' Mother?" Maybe he wasn't marrying Stephanie but that was probably more her idea than his, Jackie decided hostilely.

"Don't be sarcastic, Jacqueline. It isn't becoming. With your attitude, no wonder you haven't married."

"I must be getting better," Jackie muttered. "You've quit being nice to me. Perhaps I should have a relapse."

"Don't you dare. Now, let's see, what else do I know about your young man . . .?"

"He isn't *my* young man, Mother," she said through clenched teeth.

"Well, at any rate, I was told he had become much more active in the family corporations. And generously involved with charity work. Why, I don't believe I could even begin to name them all."

"Mother, how on earth can you know all this?"

"Are you doubting my veracity?"

"Never," Jackie replied wryly. "I just wondered *how* you found out all that. Surely not from the tabloids."

"You see, Jacqueline, it's really quite simple. You know my friend, Fern? The one I went to school with?"

"Yes, Mother. I know Fern. You used to try to make me date her horrid son, Eddie."

"Yes, I remember. Such a stubborn girl you always were. Incidentally, Edward is a very successful business-man on Wall Street now. Owns a yacht and three Mercedes. He slimmed down nicely and his complexion cleared up beautifully."

"So I'll eat my heart out, but what has this to do with your information on Giles Hafferty?"

"Fern's older sister, Marguerite, lives in Boston. Now Marguerite doesn't really know the Hafferty's well, but Marguerite's best friend's cousin is Anne Hafferty's best friend. And Anne Hafferty told her best friend that Giles had changed so much it was almost alarming. And Anne's friend told her cousin who told Marguerite who told Fern who told me because she knew I was interested. So that's how I know."

Jackie couldn't help but laugh at the roundabout tale, but her laugh wasn't too jovial. It never was anymore.

"Jackie, when are you going to quit being stubborn?" her mother asked softly.

Jackie looked at her in surprise.

"You think I'm a featherbrain, that I'm old-fashioned and have no idea what really goes on in the world. Well, you're my daughter and you can't fool me entirely. You are in love with Giles Hafferty and that's exactly what has been behind this 'illness' of yours. Perhaps you don't even realize how wrong you are in running away from a man you obviously care for. I'm sure you had your differences. But if you miss him so much you've nearly ruined your health, then why be so stubborn? Can't something be done? You didn't ask my advice, but I'm giving it. Go to him, Jackie."

All of this was the last thing Jackie had expected from her mother. Suddenly her defenses crumbled and she was being held in her mother's arms and soothed like a twelve-year-old with her first tragic crush. "But, Momma, what if he doesn't want me anymore?" she sobbed.

"We all take chances from time to time. If the stakes are worth the risk, that is."

"Well, I still have a couple of weeks left. I guess Marcus and I will go home to Biloxi and think it over."

"You do that, dear. And don't let too much pride stand in your way. Pride isn't much company in bed at night."

"Mother, really . . ." Jackie said, laughing amid her tears.

"Well, it isn't, is it?"

"No," her daughter agreed with a rueful shake of her head, "not much company at all."

Jackie thought about going to Boston. But that frightened her. The idea of standing at the huge doors of that brownstone and possibly facing rejection had little appeal. She thought about calling Giles, but what she had to say would be so difficult over the telephone. And it could also bring instant rejection. Thus what she ended up doing was taking a coward's way out. She wrote him a letter:

Dearest Giles,

There's a foolish woman in Mississippi who still loves you and misses you terribly. A woman who remembers you with kindness and hopes you remember her the same way. If you can forgive my stubbornness, please let me know.

All my love,
Jackie

Four days later a letter came Special Delivery.

My Jacqueline,

Some things are so very hard to say in person. Dramatic pronouncements sound better on paper. I won't pretend I wasn't hurt and angry when you left Massachusetts, for I was. It took quite some time for me to see things in the proper perspective. When my memory returned as fully as I suppose it ever will, I saw my life for what it was. I couldn't keep on being Mark, and as Giles, this life was all I'd ever known. At first, I saw no harm in it. Perhaps, for the most part, there is no *harm* as such. Yet after you and Marcus were gone, I gradually saw things differently. I kept remembering you and how you worked with the indigent patients, with the children in the free clinic. And I knew you would have been kind to me, done something for the poor John Doe, even if we hadn't fallen in love. And thus I knew you were right about that much . . . you couldn't give it up to float around on a yacht all day doing nothing.

Knowing you has enriched my life immeasurably. All that I know of goodness, purity, and love has come to me from you like a gift from God. How on earth could I ever remember you any other way than with kindness?

Love,
Giles

By the time she finished the letter, her eyes were blinded by tears. The words were beautiful, yet nowhere did he say, "Come to me. I still want you in my life." The letter was just a beautiful and kind brush-off. By waiting too long, she had lost him.

She put the letter down on the antique table in the living room and walked to the kitchen. Perhaps she would have a cup of hot tea for solace, though she doubted that solace was possible at the moment.

On entering the room, she gasped. Bigger than life, Giles was waiting for her there. He looked marvelously healthy and handsome in his brown wool slacks and cream-colored sweater. She stood staring at him as if stunned.

"Special Delivery," he said softly. "Letter by the front door, me by the back door."

In a flash, Jackie was in his arms, a ship safely in the harbor after a long and terrible journey on tempestuous seas.

"I've been such a fool," she said. "There are things I can do in the East that are as important as those I do here. And I have to be with you. I know that now."

"There was wrong on both sides, love. My life has been rather shallow. I don't think I fully realized that until I saw it through your eyes."

"It wasn't *that* bad," she admitted slowly. "In looking back, I can see I overreacted to that drug-oriented party. It just took me by surprise, I suppose. Even without participating in it, I don't like to be around that sort of thing. Yet I know I don't have the right to judge your friends. Or to choose them. There I was . . . wanting you to accept me as I was, letting me practice my profession when and how I pleased, and all the while, I was more or less saying you couldn't be yourself."

Giles's arms tightened around her and she felt his fingers catch in the strands of her hair as he smoothed it. "Ah, Jackie, you read my Special Delivery letter. What else can I say? Some of those people will always be my friends. I've known them all my life, and having recovered that life, I can't turn my back on it entirely. What I am doing is living it with some responsibility now. I wasn't even aware what was going on within our own companies; some of the policies were atrocious. So you should see me now. I'm a regular, hardworking son-of-a-gun. Not everything has been changed yet, but at least I'm trying. Curiously enough, I enjoy it. When I was very young, everyone around me seemed to assume I wouldn't work. After all, my father never had."

"You don't have to change to please me, Giles."

"I'm not. Believe it or not, all this hasn't been to get you back. After our encounter in New York, I was sure you'd had enough of me permanently. You sounded, acted, so cool and self-sufficient."

"You forget," she pointed out, "that you had a very attractive young woman with you. I had reason to believe I'd been replaced."

He laughed and held her at arm's length, gazing fondly into her face. "No way. If I've learned anything in all this time apart, it's that you're quite definitely irreplaceable."

"I'm glad."

They sat for a while drinking hot tea and making

plans. Jackie told him about her illness and forced vacation.

"So many times," she finished, "I wanted to call you, go to you. Then I would remember your alleged alliance with Stephanie. If you had found someone else, I had no right to intrude."

"And so many times," he said, "I wanted to approach you, to *beg* you really. Then I would recall your coldness when we met in New York and it would chill my blood."

"What a pair of idiots."

"Yep," he agreed, kissing her across the table. "At least that's all behind us now. Woe be unto anyone who ever tries to dissever us again."

"Tell me, Giles," she asked almost shyly, "would you have ever given in if I hadn't written to you?"

"Undoubtedly."

"You sound very sure."

"I am. You see, it was becoming *harder* to stay away from you, not easier. Time wasn't healing anything at all. I kept turning down dates and invitations and everyone kept telling me I'd get over you. At first, I believed them. After a while, I knew I never would. You're my once-in-a-lifetime love."

"Same here. Only at least you didn't have to suffer through thinking I'd found someone else."

"It was just as bad in a way, though, to think you were so strong and self-sufficient that you didn't need me in your life."

"Well, I've told you exactly how self-sufficient I ended up being. On a hospital bed with tubes running into my veins because I'd been too dumb to take care of myself."

"From now on out, we'll have each other. That's not to

say we won't have our ups and downs. I'm afraid we're both a bit on the stubborn side . . ."

"Who, *me*?" she asked in mock surprise, lifting up her eyebrows.

"Yes, you," he replied with a laugh, dropping a kiss onto the tender flesh of her palm. "Anyway, these strong wills of ours are bound to clash at times. But nothing is really going to matter except being together, right?"

"Right," she vowed. "By the way," she said, looking about at her kitchen, "I never thanked you for the remodeling you had done on this place. The people you hired did an excellent job. Still, I think *this* is my favorite room, because you did it yourself. And you're right about keeping it, even after we move to Boston. We should keep it for vacations, and for sentimental reasons."

"The kitchen is nice," Giles said. "Excellent workmanship, that's for sure. But I don't believe it's my favorite room."

"Then what is your favorite room?" Jackie asked, though she knew what his answer would be.

"Come on," he replied, wrinkling his nose impishly, "and I'll show you."

She laughed, but got up to go with him, suddenly finding it odd that, after such a long separation, they had sat and talked so calmly and so long instead of immediately making love. She said as much to Giles and he told her, "I suppose we aren't as impatient because we know we have the rest of our lives. Always before, we were experiencing something we feared could be taken away from us at any moment."

"And now no one can. Not ever." She smiled with contentment at her own words.

"That's right. Not ever."

When they reached the base of the stairs, he stopped, laughed, and swooped her up into his arms. As he carried her up the grand and carpeted stairway, Jackie felt like Scarlett O'Hara and Annabel Lee rolled into one. Only this time Rhett wouldn't walk out and she had no intention of letting herself be shut away in a tomb by the sounding sea.

But when Giles's lips met hers and she melted into the glory and fire of their reunion, she felt like no one at all except herself. And that was the way it should be.

RAPTURE ROMANCE

*Provocative and sensual,
passionate and tender—
the magic and mystery of love
in all its many guises*

RAPTURE ROMANCE

*Provocative and sensual,
passionate and tender—
the magic and mystery of love
in all its many guises*

Great Reading from SIGNET

SIGNET Bestsellers

(0451)

- [ ] **HOME OF THE BRAVE** by Joel Gross. (122232—$3.95)*
- [ ] **THE BOOKS OF RACHEL** by Joel Gross. (095618—$3.50)
- [ ] **MAURA'S DREAM** by Joel Gross. (112628—$3.50)
- [ ] **SEVENTREES** by Janice Young Brooks. (110684—$3.50)
- [ ] **THIS NEW LAND** by Lester Goron. (094808—$2.75)*
- [ ] **HIGH DOMINION** by Janis Flores. (111060—$3.95)
- [ ] **NEVER CALL IT LOVE** by Veronica Jason. (093348—$2.25)
- [ ] **SO WILD A HEART** by Veronica Jason. (110676—$2.95)
- [ ] **WILD WINDS OF LOVE** by Veronica Jason. (119118—$3.50)*
- [ ] **THE KISSING GATE** by Pamela Haines. (114493—$3.50)
- [ ] **WHEN THE MUSIC CHANGED** by Marie D. Reno. (099656—$3.50)*
- [ ] **ALL WE KNOW OF HEAVEN** by Sandee Cohen. (098919—$2.75)†
- [ ] **COVENANT WITH TOMORROW** by Lester Goran. (112024—$2.95)*
- [ ] **CALL THE DARKNESS LIGHT** by Nancy Zaroulis. (092910—$2.95)
- [ ] **CHEZ CORDELLA** by Kitty Burns Florey. (112660—$2.50)*
- [ ] **THE CORMAC LEGEND** by Dorothy Daniels. (115554—$2.25)*
- [ ] **AN AFFAIR OF SORCERERS** by George Chesbro. (092430—$2.25)*

*Prices slightly higher in Canada
†Not available in Canada

Buy them at your local bookstore or use this convenient coupon for ordering.

THE NEW AMERICAN LIBRARY, INC.,
P.O. Box 999, Bergenfield, New Jersey 07621

Please send me the books I have checked above. I am enclosing $_____
(please add $1.00 to this order to cover postage and handling). Send check or money order—no cash or C.O.D.'s. Prices and numbers are subject to change without notice.

Name_____

Address_____

City _____ State _____ Zip Code _____
Allow 4-6 weeks for delivery.
This offer is subject to withdrawal without notice.

RAPTURE ROMANCE

*Provocative and sensual,
passionate and tender—
the magic and mystery of love
in all its many guises*

Coming next month

CHANGE OF HEART by Joan Wolf. Man of the world Gil Archer wanted the warmth and love that only Cecelia Vargas, his daughter's riding instructor could give. She married him for love—he taught her passion. But Gil still had to learn that love wasn't meant to be taken and ignored. Would that lesson cost him Cecelia?

EMERALD DREAMS by Diana Morgan. Suzanne Lawrence vowed she'd never again be seduced by dazzling poet/playwright Jay Monahan. No longer the innocent coed overwhelmed by his genius, she was a woman in charge of her life as a professor and critic. But one meeting made Jay her teacher again, guiding her to ecstasy, yet leaving her hungering for the truth behind his love. . .

MOONSLIDE by Estelle Edwards. Knowing she couldn't follow aristocrat Karl Hauptmann back to Germany didn't cool Melissa Merrill's desire. They only had one night, but swore they'd remember it always. Then an unexpected inheritance brought her to him. Did his intoxicating kisses hide a secret ugly enough to destroy their love?

THE GOLDEN MAIDEN by Francine Shore. Suddenly widowed, Maris Verney promised to carry on her husband's latest scientific research. Turning to marine biologist Owen Wyatt for help, she couldn't understand his stubborn opposition to her work, nor could she abandon her suspicions when his taunts turned to teasing, his coolness to caresses. How long could she resist the desire threatening her very heart and soul?

TELL US YOUR OPINIONS AND RECEIVE A FREE COPY OF THE RAPTURE NEWSLETTER.

Thank you for filling out our questionnaire. Your response to the following questions will help us to bring you more and better books. In appreciation of your help we will send you a free copy of the Rapture Newsletter.

1. Book Title:_____

Book # :_____ (5–7)

2. Using the scale below how would you rate this book on the following features? Please write in one rating from 0–10 for each feature in the spaces provided. Ignore bracketed numbers.

(Poor) 0 1 2 3 4 5 6 7 8 9 10 (Excellent)
                                    0–10 Rating

Overall Opinion of Book................ _____ (8)
Plot/Story........................... _____ (9)
Setting/Location...................... _____ (10)
Writing Style......................... _____ (11)
Dialogue............................. _____ (12)
Love Scenes.......................... _____ (13)
Character Development:
Heroine:............................. _____ (14)
Hero:................................ _____ (15)
Romantic Scene on Front Cover......... _____ (16)
Back Cover Story Outline.............. _____ (17)
First Page Excerpts................... _____ (18)

3. What is your: Education: Age:_____(20-22)

High School   ( )1   4 Yrs. College ( )3
2 Yrs. College ( )2   Post Grad   ( )4 (23)

4. Print Name:_____

Address:_____

City:_____State:_____Zip:_____

Phone # (   )_____ (25)

Thank you for your time and effort. Please send to New American Library, Rapture Romance Research Department, 1633 Broadway, New York, NY 10019.